For W.R.K. and W.L.B.,
whose most unephemeral support and advice
made this book possible.

THE GHOSTS OF
NANTUCKET

23 True Accounts
by Blue Balliett
Illustrated by George Murphy

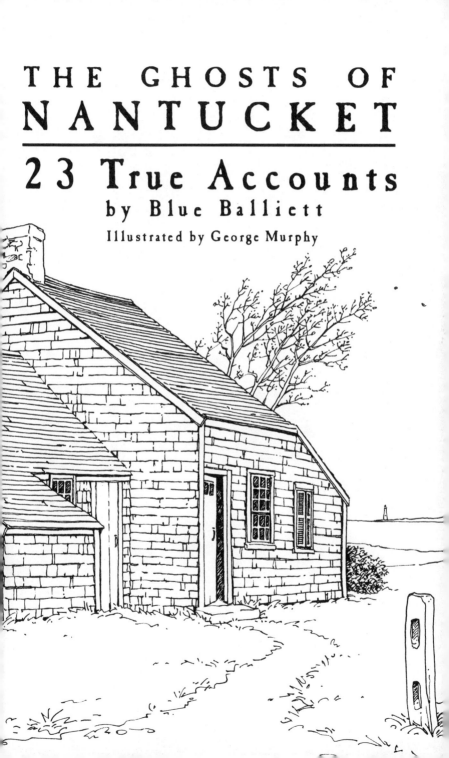

THE GHOSTS OF
NANTUCKET

CONTENTS

INTRODUCTION

Nantucket Island has 7,400 year-round residents and a sizable population of ghosts. The following stories are direct, unembellished accounts of experiences that have actually happened to summer and year-round residents. I have approached these tales as a form of oral history; I was fascinated and incredulous when I began to realize that Nantucket has a substantial number of ghosts and poltergeists, and I wanted to record, as simply and factually as possible, a sampling of this anomalous side of the island. Among those who speak are a janitor, an electrician, an antique dealer, a landscape gardener, a restoration architect, a retired restaurant owner, a housewife, a college student, a writer, a bookstore owner, a real estate agent, a hairdresser, and two children. A few are Nantucketers, most are off-Islanders, and all, interestingly enough, saw themselves as unlikely candidates for the sort of experience that happened to them.

A plump comma of land twenty-two miles off the south shore of Cape Cod in Massachusetts, Nantucket has managed to punctuate the history of the United States in a way which is all out of proportion to its diminutive size. Seventeen miles long from east to west and about three to four miles wide, the island was one of the most prosperous whaling ports in the world during the first half of the nineteenth century, and produced an impressive number of politicians, philosophers, abolitionists, suffragettes, inventors, writers, and scientists.

By 1858, when the kerosene-fueled lamp had come into widespread use, competition between Nantucket and New Bedford whalemen was becoming fierce. Quakers had lost their disciplinary grip on the island. A serious fire had destroyed most of the town's business section in 1846; a sandbar that had formed across the mouth of the inner harbor restricted shipping access, and the gold rush had lured many to California. The community was at a weak point, and as the market for whale oil and candles collapsed, Nantucket entered a period of serious decline. Businesses and families began an exodus that caused the island's population to drop from approximately ten thousand to a low of twenty-five hundred over the next forty years. Once one of the wealthiest communities in America, Nantucket became an impoverished, deserted outpost.

By the turn of the century, many of the mansions built by whaling merchants and sea captains had gap-toothed fences around their gardens and cobwebs in their windows. Grass grew up between the cobble-stones on Main Street. Paint peeled and shingles cracked. Attempts to start new industries had failed. The wharves stretched like so many leafless branches into the harbor, and the island slept.

In the early 1900s, city dwellers began to discover this tiny backwater. As a retreat from the mainstream of American life, Nantucket seemed too good to be true. It had seventy miles of beach, fields of berries and wildflowers, salty fogs, and winding, narrow streets banked by Quaker homes. It was back on the map.

The physical remnants of Nantucket's bustling heyday were unchanged; the decline of the whaling industry and the severe depression that followed had the effect of freezing almost all housing construction for over half a century. The town, through an accident of history, has one of the most extensive and remarkably preserved collections of pre-1850 buildings in America. Over the years, tourism has gradually become Nantucket's major source of income. The island is now, for better or worse, one of New England's most popular resorts; half a million people come and go during a summer, and the residential population balloons to between thirty-five and forty thousand.

Despite this influx, Nantucket has managed, at least so far, to hold onto its historical integrity and pleasant small-town atmosphere. In recent years the community has stepped up its conservation efforts and tightened restrictions on architectural styles and on growth. New buildings must reflect the standards and design precedents of older structures, and there are still no traffic lights, neon signs, fast-food chains, or franchise motels. The soft gray coloring of shingled houses dominates the town. Cobblestones and back-pocket gardens, miles of moors scribbled over with bayberry, beaches and slow dirt roads – the inevitable pressures to develop have weakened but not yet destroyed Nantucketers' reverence for old ways and

Dr. E. P. Fearing
Friends
Meeting
House
Miss Folger
R. M. Gardner

A. Dunham
Baker

Beeding Alter
Shop

OLD

Express
Office

Office

B. S. Shops
Store
Custom H

Enquirer Office

Printing Office
F. G. Kelly's Store

Allen's Block
Methodist Church
Pacific
Bank

Post Office

Town Buildings
Dr. J. B. King

L. B. Mitchell

N. Pool

G. Myrick

E. Coffin

Unit.
Ch.

J. Hinkley
C. Barnard
Easton &
A. Macy
M. Gardner
J. W. Olin

GARDNER

GUNTER

R. Smith
J. Cood

G. F. Joy
R. G. Folger

Stable

G. Coffin
Store House

G. Worth

G. Bowen

W. P. Barker
J. Gorham

MARTINS LANE

C. H. Robinson
C. Barnard

J. B. Beard

P. Macy

D. Baker

E. Jenkins

J. Wesgate
E. Starbuck Est.

H. Clapp
Candle House
W. Burgess
J. Hamblin
G. Coleman

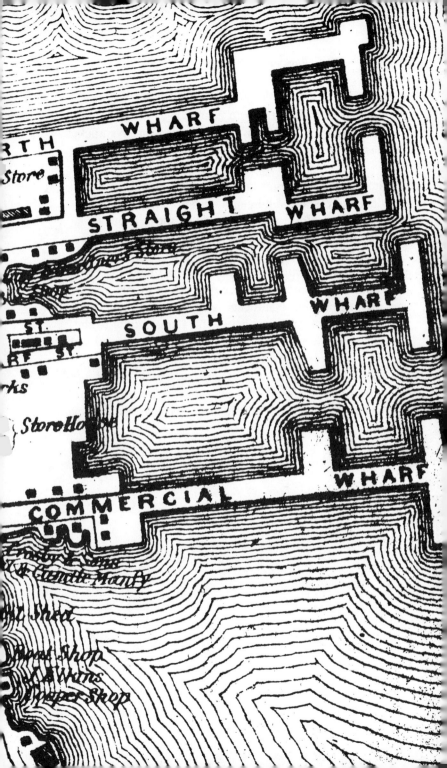

open spaces. Resistance to change is a way of life out here. Perhaps it shouldn't be surprising that Nantucket has a large subculture of ghosts.

Of the people I interviewed in gathering these stories, many did not know that paranormal disturbances are quite common here, and they were initially reluctant or embarrassed to speak about their experiences. Most prefaced their story with a phrase like, "Well, this sounds ridiculous, but . . ." Others admitted over the phone that "certain things" had gone on in their homes, but were not willing to talk about them. But then, Nantucket is a small community that gets a great deal of publicity, and I am grateful to the many people who did relate their experiences and who gave me permission to use their names and addresses in this book. Some of the names and some of the locations of the houses I have subsequently changed in order to protect the owners from any possible invasion of privacy.

THE
ABBESS

"This is about a very solid ghost. Even though it's been — oh, Lord — almost fifty years, I'd know her if I met her today."

Natalie Orloff, the kind of person who manages to look active even when supine, was curled up on the sofa in her bathing suit. The house she owns with her husband, Louis, is on the Bluff, a steep cliff rising above the ocean at 'Sconset. She is a rapid and confident talker. She gestured with her cigarette toward the window, beyond which the Sankaty lighthouse loomed in the west.

"It is that gray house across the hedge there. That's where she's been seen. My parents bought the house in '23 or '24. It had been empty during World War I, and was used by rumrunners during Prohibition. It was completely vandalized. There was a hole in the roof from a fire that someone had built in the middle of the living room. Not one piece of china or glass was intact. I was four or five when we got it, and I remember that Mother wouldn't let me walk on the floors when we went to see it. We had to climb through a window to get in, as the front door was busted. I was in Mother's arms, and she and Dad were ankle-deep in broken glass and garbage.

"Mother was wild about the location, which was the reason they bought it. Dad was planning to tear down the house and build another until he found out that the basic structure was worth a hefty $8,000. As he had only paid $1,400 for the house and land, they decided to keep the original house. It was remodeled, and new wings were added.

"Mother turned it into a beautiful, unlivable house. She had painted floors, which showed every grain of sand, and twenty-three flower vases downstairs. I remember the number because I had to change the water in them every morning.

"My bedroom was next to Mother's at the top of a flight of stairs. Dad's was around the corner and down the hall. The light from Sankaty Head flooded my room at night, and when I couldn't sleep, I counted the beams running across the ceiling. We were practically under the lighthouse, as you can see. That's an important detail, for it meant that when I opened my bedroom door at night the light flooded the stairwell also.

"One night when I was seven or eight, I heard the sound of heavy footsteps on the stairs. I was in bed, and so was Mother, but we both got up and opened our doors. Dad was in his room, but I think we both wondered if it were him, and wanted to see if anything was wrong. There, coming up the stairs, was a very pleasant-looking nun with a pug nose and a round face. She must have weighed a hundred and sixty pounds if she weighed an ounce. We were both too surprised to move, but I don't remember feeling particularly scared.

She wasn't in the least bit like a ghost, and I don't think the thought even crossed my mind until several minutes later. She had a self-assured, friendly air. Her skirts practically brushed us as she turned the corner at the top of the stairs and started down the hall to Dad's room. Now, Dad was simply not the kind of man you would just walk in on or startle, and at that point Mother came to her senses. She blurted out, 'Oh, you can't go in *there*!' The nun paused before Dad's door, gave us a warm, broad smile, and disappeared. Dad knew nothing about this whole business the next morning, and he never did see the Abbess, as we came to call her.

"Mother began to look into the history of the house. She found out that it had been built in about 1870 by two sisters who were devout Catholics. Their name was Corbett. They were very close, and when one of them died, around 1900, the other left Nantucket and loaned the house to a Boston convent as a retreat. The nuns had the property up until the First World War, when travel costs and supply shortages probably made the house too expensive to use. Some of the islanders my mother talked to said that they remembered seeing nuns down on the beach at 'Sconset. I guess the nuns were considered something of an oddity. She also found out, by describing the woman we saw that night to a neighbor, that she was dressed as a mother superior.

"I have never had the shadow of a doubt about having seen the Abbess. She had such an amiable air that it was only the fact that she was a phenomenon I didn't understand, and one that my parents obviously didn't either, that terrified me. She looked as solid as anyone I've ever known, and a good deal nicer than many.

"My mother saw her on several occasions, and I saw her once more. I was twelve at the time, and had a friend staying for the night. The two of us were sleeping in the big bed in my father's room. We woke up in the night to see the Abbess standing at the foot of the bed, smiling down at us. Predictably, we started in on preadolescent shrieks and giggles, and dove under the sheets. By the time we stuck our heads out, she was gone.

"When I was in my teens, I would often come downstairs to find a date, who had been waiting politely in the living room, looking dazed. In fact, he would be paralyzed. The problem was usually that he had been watching objects move independently around the room. A picture would be straightened, an ashtray centered on a table, or a bouquet ruffled, and always by an unseen hand. I have to admit, when I was dropped off by my date late at night, I got very good at zooming up the stairs in no time flat. I could have made some track records. The thought of meeting the Abbess in the dark wasn't appealing.

"I had one more experience with the Abbess – or at least I think it was she; I never actually saw who it was. One evening in 1947, my friend Marjorie Benchley and I were having a drink alone together in the house. We hadn't seen each other for five or six years because of the war. We were chatting about personal things when someone came into the room and sat down on a chair. Now, we couldn't see anything, and the cushions weren't depressed, but there was no question about it. We both knew from looking at each other that we were feeling the same thing. We couldn't remember anything that we really wanted to discuss, so we made ridiculous small talk for about half an hour, hoping that whoever had seemingly joined us would leave.

"Finally the situation became unbearable, and I said to Marj, 'Don't you think we need another drink?' She came into the kitchen with me, and after a whispered consultation, we decided to go back and wait it out. We took our drinks back into the living room. Whoever had been with us was still there. About twenty minutes later, this presence got up and walked out of the room. I can't tell you how we both knew precisely when it came and went, for I have no idea, but the closest I can get to describing that feeling is by telling you to imagine someone coming quietly into a room where you're sitting alone reading. Before anything has been said, you know that someone is in the room. Your senses seem to be telling you that there's another person near. It's a familiar feeling, probably just some form of convenient animal radar.

"That was the last experience I had with the Abbess before we sold the house in 1950. Mother had one kind of taste and I had another; I wasn't about to run around all summer sweeping up after sandy feet. So now Louis and I have this house next door. I'd love to ask the present owners of the house whether they've ever seen the Abbess, but I don't want to scare them. People have funny reactions to these things.

"This is just an aside, but I had one other experience with a ghost on Nantucket. In 1945, I was renting a little cottage in 'Sconset called the Brig. My husband was away most of the summer, so I was alone with my five-year-old son. I would be busy doing something in the house and would suddenly get the feeling that someone was watching me. There, outside one of the ground-floor windows, would be a sharp-faced little old lady. I saw her a number of times, always in broad daylight. She was absolutely solid. Her clothes were dark and unfamiliar to me, and she always had a bonnet on. I don't remember if it was in the Quaker style; I just remember the bonnet strings under her chin. As soon as we would catch each other's eyes, she would dart away, moving much faster than was humanly possible, and vanish. Something about her expression made me think of a shy person who was snooping, and I would almost feel embarrassed to 'catch' her looking in. I saw her inside only once. I walked into the living room in mid-afternoon, and she was sitting in a chair. Again, she was a three-dimensional, seemingly living figure, and there was nothing misty or ghostlike about her body. She gave me a quick defiant look then – *pffft!* – she disappeared. She was there one moment and simply not the next. When I looked at the empty chair, the cushions were still puffed up.

"But that's another experience. This island, as I'm sure you know, is loaded with ghosts. If someone like me has seen them, they have to be all over."

Mr. and Mrs. Julius Jensen bought the house from the Orloffs. Mr. Jensen's mother, who is no longer alive, saw the Abbess in the early 1950s. His mother, he said, was not the kind of person to imagine things. She had been a frontier nurse, and was an exceptionally fearless character.

Mr. Jensen's mother had seen a large, heavy woman in a nun's habit on the stair landing. She wasn't able to make out the features of the face, for the head was draped with a loose, shroudlike piece of material. The figure seemed to be giving off very cold air.

Mr. Jensen had listened with interest to his mother's experience, but didn't think much of it; she was getting rather old. And he had never, until his conversations with me, heard about Mrs. Orloff's tales of the Abbess.

Makaala and Liz Wolven spent a winter in the house not too many years ago. They had three dogs at the time. Mrs. Wolven said that she liked the house, but that her dogs were never comfortable there. She and her husband knew nothing about the Abbess.

The dogs refused to go into the bedroom at the head of the stairs. To conserve heat, the Wolvens generally kept the upstairs doors tightly shut, but when they would return after being out, the door and one window in this room would always be open. Mrs. Wolven said that the dogs had an infuriating number of accidents in that house, and never wanted to stay there alone.

Mrs. Wolven mentioned that she and her husband would sometimes have the strange feeling of being watched by someone in the stairwell or in that problematic bedroom. They did their best to ignore this sensation.

The Abbess was last seen in the early '70s. A young couple, spending the winter in Sea Watch, looked out the window one stormy day in January to see a nun standing on the front lawn in full regalia, her habit billowing and snapping in the wind. They were puzzled at this strange sight, but when she vanished into thin air they were petrified. Not knowing what else to do, they called the police. The officer at the desk put them in touch with Nathaniel Benchley, then living year-round on Nantucket. Mr. Benchley and his wife Marjorie had spent many summers in 'Sconset, and he was able to explain the story of the house to them. Unfortunately, he was unable, years later, to remember their name.

T H E
S H I M M E R I N G
B U B B L E

The 1800 House on Mill Street is located in an old section of the town. The house has no sidewalk in front, and sits, plain and stiff-backed, on a little rise a couple of feet from the macadam. It has a rough fieldstone foundation and a steep flight of stairs which rise sharply to the front door.

The building gives off a feeling of separateness that is not welcoming. Many of Nantucket's historic houses seem graciously openhearted in their old age, but the 1800 House just doesn't. It is alive with the arthritic sounds of old wood; pops, ticks, and creaks are audible in every room. The building was restored by the Nantucket Historical Association in the early '50s, and is an early example of a form of construction popular on Nantucket in the first half of the nineteenth century. A central door with two equidistant windows on either side added a certain formality that the earlier lean-to houses never had. One opens the front door into a small stair hall leading into parlors on the left and on the right. The effect is like that of holding a stick in a rapid stream; the stairs shoot upward from the front hall, and the passage forks around the stairwell, meeting again in the large keeping room. The keeping room, where most of the cooking and living was once done, has five doors: one on either side of the fireplace, opening into each of the front parlors, one to a borning room on the west, one to a weaving room on the east, and one to a summer kitchen in back. The door that plays a part in this story is the parlor door on the west end of the keeping room, near the door to the borning room.

Nineteenth-century families spent most of their winter months in the keeping room. With its large hearth and southern exposure, it must have been the warmest and most welcoming room in the house. The borning room was used for just that purpose. Not much bigger than a cubbyhole, it was easy to keep warm in the winter, and was convenient not only for giving birth but for taking care of sick children or the elderly. There are five large rooms upstairs.

In midwinter of 1972, electrician Parker Gray was hired to install a complex alarm system in the building. The alarm system consisted of infrared and ultrasonic rays, backed up with magnetic contacts fastened onto all of the doors and windows. When the system is on, an alarm goes off in the police station if a window or door is opened, or if any solid object passes through the infrared or ultrasonic beams.

From the time it was first activated, the alarm went off between seven and quarter to eight every Tuesday and Thursday night. Each time the police hurried to the house they found it quiet and undisturbed, with the exception of the ground-floor latch door connecting the west parlor and the keeping room. This door, which was wired with magnetic contacts, would be found open.

As the electrician, Parker Gray was in an awkward position. By the fifth week of false alarms, the police and the Historical Association began to wonder if someone was playing an ingenious trick, or if Parker had indeed installed the alarm system properly. No one could think of a plausible explanation. Parker disconnected the magnetic contact so that no alarm would go off. The door would still be open on Wednesday and Friday mornings. The other four doors leading out of the keeping room were all wired to the alarm system, and all remained closed.

Parker was understandably upset by this inexplicable problem. He wondered at first if a passing truck (very unlikely on Mill Street in midwinter) or an airplane could be jiggling the door latch loose. He tried walking heavily and then jumping up and down on either side of the door to see if the latch would bounce free. No luck. The latch itself was set in a cradle nearly a half-inch deep, a type of fitting that is really too secure to be jolted open by a vibration. The only reasonable conclusion was that the latch was actually being lifted.

The possibility of a ghost in the house was not mentioned. Everyone concerned had heard about "presences" in various Nantucket homes, but no one wanted to admit the existence of a ghost that opened doors. As a last resort, Parker took his assistant to the house between 6:30 and quarter to seven one Tuesday night, and they turned off the alarm, entered quietly, and stood out of sight of the troublesome door in a small storage closet around the corner from the west parlor. The door to the storage room was left open.

They waited there for half an hour or so. Parker's assistant was just whispering to him that this was a "helluva way to spend a cold February night" when they heard the latch click. Parker, in recounting the story, said that he wanted to roar at the way his skeptical assistant blanched and rushed out the front door, slamming it behind him. Parker could hear his boots thumping off at a run down the quiet street; the man didn't even wait outside in the company truck.

When no further sounds came from the next room, Parker stepped out of the storage room and peered around the doorway leading into the west parlor. The door to the keeping room had indeed swung open, and he saw ("it seemed like an eternity, although it was probably only fifteen to thirty seconds") something moving slowly toward him. As he put it, "there was definitely something there," coming through the open door, and it wasn't a sight he had ever seen before. He described it as looking like a shimmering soap bubble the size of a basketball; it was pulsing, moving gently in and out in all directions. He used his hands to show me its shape, and said that it was about as translucent as light wax paper. It floated past him, through the west parlor door, within one or two feet of where he was standing. He could feel an "extraordinary and really horrible coldness" that seemed to surround the bubble. He said that he felt nervous but for some reason not really scared by the approach of this strange "object," for it was traveling through the west parlor in an unhurried, deliberate way that didn't seem to have anything to do with his presence. In retrospect, he says, he doesn't know why he was so sure of this, or why he was so relaxed about standing in the path of this bizarre thing. Moving evenly at the pace of a slow

The door to the keeping room had indeed
swung open, and he saw something moving
slowly toward him through the open door.

walk, the bubble went past the storage closet and through the front hall and disappeared up the stairs. Parker did not follow it.

He told his story to the president of the Historical Association, and together they decided to fasten the door with an eyehook the following day. The hook and eye were attached to the west-parlor side of the door, thus preventing one from opening the door from inside the keeping room. There has been no trouble since.

The house has changed hands only five times since 1807. Shortly before the house was built, the area was described in local records as "a tract of land in the Richard Gardner share westward of Stephen Chase's house." The house first appeared on record in a deed dated February 1807, when a housewright by the name of Richard Coleman sold the homestead to Jeremiah Lawrence, "High Sheriff for the County" and a prominent town official of his day. The house was probably built shortly after Coleman bought the land in 1801.

In 1856 Jeremiah's widow, Eunice, sold the house to Love Calder; James Monroe Bunker (schoolteacher, notary public, and civil engineer) bought the house in 1865 and lived there with his family for thirty-eight years, selling it to Leonora E. James in 1903. Mrs. James, a peppery and outspoken member of the community, lived in the house for forty-eight years, many of them spent with her husband and children, and sold the house to Louise Anderson Melhado in 1951. Mrs. Melhado gave it to the Historical Association shortly after she bought it, and the house is open to the public during the summer months.

Unfortunately, little is known of the Lawrence or Bunker families. Nor did Mrs. James leave behind any diaries or papers that might have shed light on the existence of the mysterious bubble. Each of the three families spent close to half a century in the building; perhaps one of the former owners is still, in spirit, making the nightly rounds.

SOMETHING
EVIL IN
THE ATTIC

"The house is on Cliff Road. I don't feel you should use our name, but I'll tell you the story.

"My husband and I bought the house in 1960. It wasn't old; it was built in the '20s, and had been owned by only one family. The man who built it and lived there for all those years was no longer alive when we bought it, but we don't know of anything terrible ever having happened in the place.

"It all began with something our ten-year-old daughter, Janet, either imagined or saw. Her bedroom was upstairs, opposite the door to the attic. The children spent hours playing in the attic. It was their territory, a place where they set up forts and clubs and arranged things the way they wanted them.

"Janet was a little afraid of that door at night; she was a sensitive, imaginative child who had awful nightmares for years, and was very scared of the dark. She had outgrown most of those fears by the time she was nine or ten, but if anyone were to be scared by a ghost, it would certainly be she. As she tells it, she was reading in bed one night and looked up to see the attic door, which was always closed at bedtime, wide open. A shimmery, insubstantial figure of a man was standing in the doorway. Janet was petrified, and must have looked it. She says she isn't too clear about what happened next, but the figure communicated to her, either silently or in words, 'Please don't worry. Don't be scared. I don't mind if you can't look at me.' The apparition calmed Janet by letting her know that he wasn't bad and wasn't going to hurt her. He told her that his name was George. I gather that they sort of made friends.

"Now, Janet is the first to say that she may very well have imagined this entire experience. She wasn't asleep, however, and remembers the feeling of George's presence, the feeling of losing her fear of him and of realizing he was a kind person. (George, incidentally, was not the name of the man who had owned the house before us.) She may have told the other children about this strange man the next day, but she didn't mention him to me or her father for some time. When she did, it came up casually in a conversation as something curious that she had seen one night. She was no longer spooked by him at all.

"That was the only time she saw the apparition. About four years later we had a bad fire in the attic. One of the children had left a light burning too close to the wall, and the dry wood went up in flames. Fortunately, we were home at the time, and the damage was minimal compared to what it might have been.

"After the fire, the attic needed extensive repair work, and my husband and I decided to turn it into a master bedroom. The children didn't mind, for they had more or less outgrown it as a play space. We fixed it up and began using it ourselves. That was when the trouble began.

"I was up there one day and suddenly felt something extremely frightening coming over me. I can't be precise about it, for I still don't have the faintest idea what it was. It pressed toward me and literally paralyzed me with fear. I couldn't move or talk or call out for help. It was if it was trying to suffocate me, take me over, pull me out of my body: I really didn't know whether I could survive it that first time. It was invisible and silent. When I got my voice back I let out what I guess was a strangled-sounding squawk. I was very badly shaken.

"I've heard a number of ghost stories about Nantucket homes, but I've never heard of anything this bad occurring in any other house on the island. I don't know if one would even call this a ghost; I could only think of it as an utterly terrifying, malevolent force.

"I had a number of these attacks in our bedroom over the next few years. One even happened when my husband was in the room with me and wasn't aware that it was going on until I had broken out of it. I'm not at all the type of person to have mediumistic or other-worldly feelings; my husband, too, was scared and worried by these invisible assaults. We didn't move out of the bedroom, although perhaps we should have. We did, however, talk about selling the house.

"One of my greatest fears was that this force would try to harm one of our children or someone visiting us. Our son Paul's fiancée did have an experience very similar to mine one night. This was the only time that something happened to someone other than me, and the only time it happened outside of our attic bedroom.

"Paul and Emily were sitting downstairs after the

rest of us had gone up. I remember that when I tried to put the garbage out that night after dinner I found that the back door wouldn't open. Both my son and my husband tried to free it, with no success. We had never had this problem before, but we didn't think much of it and went to bed, leaving Emily and Paul alone.

"It was close to midnight when they heard the back door open. After a short pause, they heard someone in heavy boots crossing the kitchen. Both were startled and looked toward the door. There was no one there. The footsteps continued to move at a thudding, deliberate pace, straight toward where they were sitting in the living room. They didn't have much time to react, and I guess neither moved. The steps walked right up to Emily. She was then utterly overwhelmed in a way that sounded very similar to my experiences. Paul tried to help her, sitting by her for over an hour before she came out of it. She was paralyzed, frozen by this consuming, terrifying pressure. She was extremely upset, and I remember her saying the next morning that she didn't think she could stay on in the house.

"The tide turned with something quite funny. I came to open up the house one summer with a Bulgarian woman who was going to be working for us. She was a cheery, salt-of-the-earth sort of person. We had brought along the family dog, a toy beagle terrier. From downstairs in the kitchen, I whistled to the dog, for I had put out his food. He didn't come and didn't come. I looked around, calling his name, and then heard whimpering coming from upstairs. I found the dog just inside the open door to our bedroom. He was whining and prancing in front of something that was blocking the doorway and wouldn't let him get by. I couldn't see anything, but after my own experiences, I was scared to reach into the room. I was standing in the hall wondering what on earth to do, when our housekeeper came up behind me. My heart sank, for I was afraid that once she found out there was something bad in the house she would quit on the spot. But all she said was 'Ghost, huh?' and turning her back to the open door gave whatever was blocking it a great bump with her fanny. She stepped in, scooped up the dog and brought him downstairs for his supper. It didn't faze her in the least.

"That taught me something. I was sitting in our bedroom at my desk one day when I heard a pop. It was the rod holding the curtains on one window. The curtains fell to the floor. A couple of seconds later there was another pop, and then another. By then, three curtains were down. Remembering our housekeeper's attitude, I said out loud 'All right, so I need some new curtains! Fine!' With that, all of the other curtains were ripped off and thrown to the floor. The fabric was old and faded in places, and it was indeed time to replace the curtains, so the next day I bought some Liberty print at Nantucket Looms and made new panels. And strangely enough, ever since then I've had the feeling that the malevolent spirit, presence, or whatever, is gone from the house.

"I guess it's possible that George, Janet's supposed apparition, felt that the attic was his territory and was trying to chase us out by attacking me. But George had seemed quite harmless and friendly, and I felt that whatever went after Emily and me was really evil. Those moments of terror were far worse than anything else I have ever known."

HEAVEN IS
TWO WEEKS
AWAY

"Powell. We're talking about Jason Powell," Mark Schofield said, crossing his legs and settling back in his chair. Mark's wife, Grace, poured three glasses of lemonade.
He continued, "My former wife bought our house on Bloom Street from Jason Powell, who was a psychiatrist in New York City. I have a landscaping business, and worked for him for ten years before he sold the house. He was a good man, but he had a difficult marriage and an unlucky life, and he loved his gin. He moved off-island for good several years ago, and had a serious hip operation. He was mixing his booze with painkillers, I guess, and he died in his sleep. No one knew the circumstances. He was alone at the time."

Mr. Schofield's comfortably creased face is accented by his eyes, which are an authoritative, almost audible blue.

"About a week after Powell died, I was awakened at 3 A.M. We keep a night light in the bathroom adjacent to our bedroom, and by its light I could see someone

35

in a long granny nightgown walking by the bed toward
the bathroom. I automatically stretched my foot out to
check for Grace. She was fast asleep next to me. I
hate the dark, and snapped the light on in a hurry.
Whatever it was disappeared. It wasn't until some time
later that I remembered that Powell used to wear those
old-fashioned flannel nightshirts in the winter. The
next night, at the same time, I was awakened again. I
felt my face lifted up and turned toward the ceiling,
and there was Jason's face above me. He was smiling,
as if to reassure me. I was terrified, and turned on the
light and woke Grace up. Again, there was nothing
there.

"The third night, I was woken up again at 3 A.M.,
this time by a loud thumping in the bathroom. Grace
was still asleep. I listened for a while, then got myself
together, went to the bathroom, and slowly opened the
door. As I snapped on the light the noise stopped and
a cold wind poured past me out the door. The window
had been shut all night and was still tightly closed. I
have to admit I was scared; I had never had an
experience like that before.

"This next part sounds funny, but I didn't know
what else to do. In the morning, I went all through the
house talking to Jason. 'You old bastard,' I said, 'I know
you're here and I know you're not happy with what's
going on.' You see, we were friends, and I know he
loved life and didn't mean to kill himself. Many people
thought it was a suicide, but I'm sure it was not. As I
see it, I might have been a kind of interpreter for him.
He was tormented, I think, by the way he had died,
and needed to get in touch with someone who was his
friend. At any rate, I walked all through the house, just
talking to him, and he never came back.

"I've thought about that experience a lot since then. It relieved me in a way; no matter what anyone says, I now have no doubt about a world beyond. When you talk about ghosts, you're dealing with a side of life that isn't scientific or logical – but then, dying and disappearing for good doesn't seem very logical either. When my first wife died, many years ago, I remember feeling that she was back in the house at Bloom Street, as if to say that she was still with me, for about a week after she died. Another week later, I was just as sure she was gone to wherever you do go. Powell also made his appearance within two weeks after his death. There seems to be a transition period. It's as if heaven is two weeks away."

SETH

The Unitarian Church on Orange Street was built in 1809 as the Second Congregational Meeting House Society Church. Its bell was brought from Lisbon, Portugal, in 1812 by Captain Thomas Cary. The tower has seen three clocks: the first was installed at the time of construction, the second in 1823, and the present one in 1881. In 1884, the interior was modernized by the architect F.B. Coleman, who set in the tall, elegant, side windows, and added a vestry and kitchen downstairs. The *trompe l'oeil* wall painting is attributed to Carl Wendte, an artist who had previously decorated the Treasury Building in Washington.

The church has a cheerful, proud, shingled countenance. Its classical structure brings to mind the child's game, "Here is the church, here is the steeple, open the doors . . ." The famous steeple, located on the front of the building, is a landmark visible from five miles at sea. The bell, now electric, strikes every hour around the clock, with an additional fifty-two strokes for reveille at 7:00 A.M. for lunch at noon, and for curfew at 9:00 P.M.

Francis and Ellen Morgan have been the
janitor and housekeeper for the church since 1968. Mr.
Morgan, at work in the church one morning,
related the following story:

"I was in here alone one winter day six or seven
years ago, and was working around in the vestry when
two kids I knew tapped on the window over there,
wanting to come in. It was a cold, blustery day, with
snow outside, kind of nasty, so I let them in. I was in
the kitchen, where I keep all my tools and such, and I
could hear the kids upstairs runnin' and hootin' and
dashin' back and forth the way kids do, and then I
heard them clattering down the stairs and running out
the front door. It slammed shut. Five or ten minutes
later they were back tappin' on the window. When I
let them back in I asked, 'Why'd you go out? You
knew the door was locked from outside.' And they
said, 'Why, a man upstairs chased us out; he didn't
want us up there, and scared us.' I knew there was no
one upstairs, but I didn't say anything to the kids, not
wanting to really frighten them. I think Seth, as we call
the spirit in this church, has an aversion to kids gettin'
into deviltry. It's not really surprising, for in the old
days most folks were very rigid about those things, and
people – especially children, who were supposed to be
mindful of their elders – were expected to adhere to
certain codes of behavior. This spirit probably
disapproves of someone runnin' and shriekin' around in
the House of God.

"A couple of months after that, when it was a little
warmer out, I brought my young grandson here one
day. I took him up to the altar to show him where our
minister stands, and he wanted to know if the big
Bible there was God's book, and if the seat was God's

seat. My grandson was asking all sorts of regular little-boy questions. Then suddenly he got very quiet and just kept starin' at the pulpit. He said, 'I don't like that man. I don't like the way he looks.' Knowing we were alone in the church, I said, 'What man?' He pointed to the pulpit. I couldn't see anything, but I didn't tell him that, and we just went and did something else.

"Of course, you know about what happened with Cathy Cronin. When she was still teaching in Rhode Island, before she got her school underway here, she needed a quiet place to correct students' papers. She used to come work in the vestry, sittin' over by the windows in the brightest part of the room. One day when she got through, and was going home along the pathway outside, she heard a terrific bang against one of those windows, and looking up saw a bodiless hand waving, in a flat arc from left to right, good-bye to her.

"One morning I was working in the vestry when I heard a really hard bang on one of the windows over there. This had happened to me twice before. If someone had actually gone up to the window and hit it that hard, I'm sure the blow would have driven the sash out and smashed the glass. So I said out loud, 'Now, be careful, or you'll break it.' It hasn't happened again.

"Susie Jarrell, the organist, often comes in here alone, and she has said she's heard things in the organ loft upstairs. Once when she was downstairs practicing in the vestry, she felt something pullin' her toward the corner over there, near the windows. She kept looking over, but didn't see anything. I know just what kind of feeling she's talking about; there are times when I'm in here cleaning or puttering around, and just know I'm not alone. You can feel a definite presence.

Second Congregational
Meeting House Society
Unitarian Universalist

The church has a cheerful, proud, shingled
countenance.

"Ted Anderson, our minister, came to the church in 1972. After he'd been here a short while, we told him that there was a spirit in the building. He laughed, at the time. But one evening shortly after his arrival here, he was upstairs alone, just strolling back and forth in the aisle, putting his sermon together, when he heard the repeated sound of a pencil dropping. He told us about it. My wife and I have heard that many times. The first time it happened to us, we were working in different parts of the building, and each thought the other was dropping something over and over. Finally she called out to me, 'Would you quit droppin' that pencil! It's makin' me irritated!' The upstairs is all carpeted, you know, up and down the aisle and between the pews. You shouldn't be hearing the sound of a pencil dropping on a bare floor when the floor's got a carpet on it!

"I think Seth is a nice spirit. It seems that he just gets a little restless sometimes, and that's when we hear him dropping things, or walking up and down the hallway in the vestry, for we often hear footsteps. We call the spirit Seth because Seth F. Swift, the first minister of the church, from 1810 to 1834, was at the helm here longer than anyone else. That's his portrait upstairs, painted by William Swain. His eyes follow you everywhere.

"About five years ago, I had an odd experience with a radio. Everything in the vestry had become mildewed over a damp winter; that spring I was scrubbing it all down and painting the ceiling. It was a tedious job. One day I brought a portable radio in with me, and had it on the platform up in front. It was tuned in to a station which played good, quiet, modern music, but then the announcer started playing this hard rock stuff. I didn't bother to change the channel. After a couple of minutes of that, the radio shut right off. I went up and checked the switch, but the radio was dead as a doornail, even though it had new batteries in it. Thinking that the problem might be something in the building interfering with the reception, I walked outside with the radio, and it went right back on. But as soon as I walked back inside and set it down, it clicked right off again. I picked it up, took it outside again, and it went on. I couldn't figure out what the problem was until it occurred to me that maybe Seth didn't like the music. So I switched channels until I found a nice classical station, took the radio back inside, set it down, and it played beautifully for the rest of the day. It's a funny sensation to cross paths with a spirit when you're not expectin' it, but as I see it, Seth just has certain dislikes which he won't permit in the church, and that's when he manifests himself.

"Which reminds me, last summer we had three professional painters, brothers from Hingham, painting the outside of the church. They were steeplejacks, too. They were almost through with the job, standing out in back takin' a rest, when the whole block-and-tackle rig on the roof came flying down and hit the ground between them. A step in the wrong direction, and one of them might have been killed. All three were astounded, and scared to death. The only way that rig could have fallen was if a person up there had loosened it. Those men do dangerous work, climbing around roofs and turrets and such, and are dependent on that rig to keep them from falling. It is always checked and rechecked, and there was absolutely no possibility, according to those men, that they could've been careless about it. They were so shaken up they could hardly eat dinner that night, and couldn't wait to get that job finished and leave Nantucket. They must have said or done something that made Seth furious.

"Some people have the misconception that spirits don't exist, but, especially on this island, they are sadly mistaken. I guess some people are scared or threatened by the idea of a ghost, but when I think about ghosts, I think about that statement made by a great leader of ours who said that 'there is nothing to fear but fear itself.' I think almost every old house here on Nantucket that's over a hundred years old has a spirit or two lingering on in it. My God, if everyone who had a ghost in their house was willin' to talk about it, you'd never get through with your project.

"My wife and I have a ghost in our house on Prospect Street. The house was built in the 1790s, and all the doors have deep latch fittings. Sometimes we'll be sittin' alone, when everything's nice and quiet, and hear the latch being opened on one of the doors, and then see the door swing open. Those aren't fastenings that can free themselves in the way a modern door can if it's not shut properly. You really have to press down on the latch to get the door open, and if the latch isn't properly dropped when you shut the door, it won't stay closed. We've also heard someone walking down the stairs from the second floor, or a chair suddenly falling over, or a door closing firmly by itself; just funny little random happenings that we had nothing to do with. We don't mind."

O N E
S I L V E R
S P O O N

"**M**y home was built in 1746 by George Hussey as a wedding present to his daughter, Dinah, when she married Reuben Folger. In its 238 years of existence, the building has been owned by only four different families.

"I moved in thirty-one years ago and did a great deal of interior stripping, renovating, and reconstruction. It was all very exciting, for returning the house to its original condition meant getting a feeling for the people who had lived in it, too. During restoration, a roughly scrawled message was uncovered on the lintel over the keeping-room hearth. Written with chalk, using the old-fashioned *S*, it read: 'When this you see — remember me.' I've often wished I could, but there is no signature.

"Shortly after I moved in, I had gone up to bed when a neighbor called to say that there was a light on downstairs. I guess she was afraid that I might have left a candle burning. I thanked her and went down to check, only to find that the keeping room was absolutely dark. Just as I was leaving the room I felt something soft and warm brush my leg. I thought it was my dog, and clicked on a lamp. The dog wasn't in the room. When I went back upstairs I found him happily curled up on the foot of my bed.

"I had never formed much of an opinion one way or the other about ghosts, but that night I *knew* that something large and solid had brushed against me. It wasn't unpleasant, just a little odd.

"Over the years, I heard other stories about the place. Susan Sevrens, who has since passed away, once rented the house. She went home for lunch one day and walked into the keeping room only to see, in broad daylight, a woman in full colonial dress slipping out the far door. When she followed the woman, Mrs. Sevrens could find no one. As she had thought, she was alone in the house. Janie Wallach also lived here for a number of years. She told me that none of her cats would voluntarily go into the keeping room. If she carried them in, their hair would stand on end and they would scramble out of her arms.

"There is a story about this place. It involves Judith Chase, a rich Quaker who at one time owned the property. She apparently used to sit in the keeping room and count her silver every night. One evening, she found a spoon missing. She called the servant girl into the room and accused her of having taken it. Despite the girl's protestations of innocence, she was fired. The girl was apparently unable to find work after that and she starved to death. It is said to be her spirit that returns to the house.

"Now, here's a funny thing. Helen Backus Shaw, who I believe was born in the house, once told me that her grandfather, when cleaning the fireplace, found a single silver spoon hidden up on a ledge in the keeping-room chimney. I've often wondered about that one silver spoon."

A WOMAN
IN THE
FIREPLACE

Jack and Clair Vandenberg bought the house
in the spring of 1972. It was a "depressing"
house, as Mrs. Vandenberg said; it was dank
and musty and smelled of rotting wood.
They scrubbed, painted, restored, repaired, rewired,
put in new plumbing fixtures, and brought in their own
furniture. To Mrs. Vandenberg's dismay, the unhealthy
smell still clung.

Located off Orange Street on the outskirts of
town, the house was built around 1835. It is one and
three-quarter stories, shingled, and has a stone
foundation and a ridge chimney. The present chimney
is original. Heat provided by an oil furnace comes up
through floor grates downstairs, but there is no heat on
the second floor. There are four big fireplaces, two
upstairs and two down, and a gas stove in the kitchen.
A large wooden storage closet is built into the wall
next to the kitchen fireplace downstairs.

One day shortly after the family moved there,
Mrs. Vandenberg went to the storage closet for a
bucket. She was reaching toward the back of the

closet, one foot inside, when she felt a shock of panic and "absolute fear" as acute as an electrical current. She snatched her hand back, leaped out, and slammed the door. She says, quite simply, that she was overcome by something that "wasn't good" and was "active or alive" in that closet. She insists that the feeling was instinctive and in no way interpretive, and Mrs. Vandenberg is not a skittish sort of woman. Her reaction was pure reflex, for the scare was too immediate to allow time for thought.

The experience was the first of many like it that happened near the fireplaces in the house. The feeling was one of being bullied by someone; there would suddenly be "something there" in the area of one of the fireplaces. Mrs. Vandenberg noticed that the upstairs closet next to the fireplace, directly above that first-floor closet, also seemed to have its moments. The second-floor closet has a wooden door in the ceiling that opens up to an additional storage area. Several times as Mrs. Vandenberg went to get a blanket or sheets, she had a prickly sensation and a strange feeling that someone was looking down at her from behind that ceiling door.

At times, the fireplace closets felt perfectly normal, and the idea of these strange visitations appeared ridiculous. In addition, the intrusions always seemed to happen when her children and husband were not around; she began to wonder whether she was just imagining things.

When Jack had a similar experience, quite out of character for him, she was both relieved and worried. According to Mrs. Vandenberg, he has neither interest nor patience where paranormal phenomena are concerned. Nevertheless, when he was alone in the house one day, he apparently felt a rush of that same intangible threat. He later told her that he suddenly knew that there was something "pushing" at him in the house. To his own surprise, he found himself yelling, "This is our house now and you get out of here!" Husband and wife felt equally silly about their dramatic reactions, but couldn't seem to help themselves. The feeling of an intruder was unpleasant and scary.

One of the oddest details of the story is Mrs. Vandenberg's experience of an idea that "would keep forming itself" in her mind, like an irritating song heard too many times on the radio. The idea was that something abusive had happened to a twenty-eight-year-old woman in the house. The woman had black hair, wore long, dark clothes, and was very angry. The image was a specific one. Mrs. Vandenberg tried to shake the idea when it ran through her mind, and was amused by the fact that the woman seemed suspiciously like a character lifted from a bad gothic novel; but she found that the thought would return with a strange persistence.

Next to the fireplace upstairs is a heavy Empire chest of drawers that the Vandenbergs brought with them. It sits against the wall, about two and a half feet from the edge of the fireplace. The drawers have metal knobs, and are graduated in size. Mrs. Vandenberg had been hearing a very faint clinking noise, like the sound of coins or keys being jingled together, coming from the direction of the bureau. The sound was just the "tiniest vibration," and would go on for several hours at a stretch. She checked the knobs on the bureau, finding them tightly screwed on, and then tried unplugging all the electrical appliances in the house to see if the clinking was being caused by a machine or lamp. It was not. The sound was coming from one of the center drawers, and yet there was nothing in the drawer itself that could be making the noise. She tried pulling the drawer out of the bureau. If she held it tightly enough, the noise would stop, only to start again as soon as she loosened her grip. This intermittent clinking went on for two months or so, until one day she lost her temper. Feeling foolish, but too frazzled to care, she said firmly, "Now this is enough! I've really had enough!" The noise stopped abruptly, and she has never heard it again.

This shed new light on the problem. Whatever was in the house was apparently capable of interacting, for it seemed to respond to a firm reprimand. Mrs. Vandenberg had occasionally been aware of something near one of the fireplaces, something more defined and slightly firmer than the invisible feeling of threat. Although she never actually saw anything, she described it as being like "a displacement of air," comparing it to a small-scale version of the change in air pressure one feels when being passed by a car on the highway. It was a "using-up of space, as if the air in the room was being pushed toward me or around me." She felt that it was sometimes an object about her own size, and at other times something perhaps twice the size of a person. The feeling it gave was not like that of a breeze or a gust, but was simply a perceptible change in air density.

One night when she and her young son were upstairs, she distinctly heard a woman moaning, as if in pain, from inside the fireplace. Although instinctively horrified, she did everything she could to misinterpret the sound. She was reading in bed at the time, and got up and checked on her son, who was asleep in his room. That, however, was merely a gesture, for she knew that the low wailing was not one a child could make. She stuck her head out the window in the hope that the sound was coming from outside. It was not. She was sure that it wasn't the wind or an animal; it was unmistakably human.

She had found that when she thought *at* whatever it was, in a kind but firm way ("Now, we're not going to start *that* again," or, "Just stop this, right now."), the intruding presence would fade. She concentrated, and tried this with the moaning. It stopped. Aside from the intermittent clinking in the bureau, this was the only time she had heard a sound connected with the disturbance.

Gradually, the threatening presence seemed to be leaving the house, for it made itself felt less frequently, and became fainter in its manifestations. Mrs. Vandenberg observed that its disappearance involved a battle of wills. If she became even slightly panicky or tried to ignore it, it "grew stronger." She hasn't felt it for four or five years now. The dank, unhealthy smell that formerly permeated the house also faded, and finally disappeared for good. Mrs. Vandenberg says she doesn't care what the source of these disturbances was, nor does she think about it much anymore; she is just thankful that it has finally gone.

GEORGE
CUSHMAN

"**I** rented a small house on Prospect Street in the summer of 1945. The war was over, and I was there alone with my two-year-old daughter, Betsy, waiting for my husband to come back from overseas. The island was filled with young war wives at the time. Many of the houses were boarded up. We all rode bikes to and from the store, and it was unusually peaceful and quiet. The island still had the subdued feeling that it had had during the worst of the war years.

"The house is a pre-Revolutionary saltbox with two front rooms, which were once used as parlors, and a larger keeping room behind. I had set up my bed and Betsy's cot in the left parlor. At night, the street lamps illuminated the room. The house had a friendly feeling to it. Although I was only twenty-four, I never felt lonely or uncomfortable there.

"This particular experience was an isolated incident. I had spent the evening in the keeping room with a friend. We had been talking about this and that, and making argyle socks in front of the fire. My friend left at about ten o'clock and I went to bed and fell asleep immediately.

"I was awakened in the night by the thump-click sound of a latch being lifted. I turned over and saw a short, elderly man crossing the room. He had apparently just entered by the keeping-room door, for it was still swinging open behind him, and he was headed toward the other door, which opens from our bedroom into the front hall. Dressed in oilskins, he was long in the body and short in the legs. He had a swordfisherman's cap on, and was carrying a pail. He never gave any sign that he was aware of my presence, and was halfway across the bedroom, walking at a normal pace, when I said something like 'What are you doing in here?' As I spoke, he vanished.

"I knew it was only a nightmare, but I was badly shaken. I got Betsy and put her in bed with me. Curling up with the baby, I closed my eyes and eventually went back to sleep.

"In the morning I noticed that the bedroom door, which I always closed at night, was open. It's impossible for one of those deep latch fittings to open by itself. The goose flesh rose on my neck. I gathered Betsy up and went over to my neighbor's house. A sensible, brusque word or two was what I needed. Mrs. Olney Dunham was a straightforward Scandinavian woman who called a spade a spade. I told her what had happened to me, and described the little man in detail. She looked at me oddly and said, 'Why, George Cushman's been dead for years!' "

WILLIAM COFFIN'S HOUSE

The house was built in 1808. It stood at the head of Main Street, presiding over the town until 1817, when it was moved to its present location on Union Street to make way for the new Pacific National Bank building. The house belonged to William Coffin.

Mr. Coffin was a victim in the notorious 1795 robbery of the Nantucket Bank. Located where Buttner's department store now stands on Main Street, the bank was the first to be established on the island and only the third in Massachusetts. It was organized by a group of people with political and financial influence in the community. Some friction was to be expected, for the stakes were high and the founders had varying opinions on how such a business should be run. No one, however, expected a conflict such as the one that soon followed.

Less than two weeks after the bank opened, $21,000 disappeared from the vault overnight. The directors and stockholders of the bank turned against each other, and the town was wracked with backbiting

and gossip. The theft seemed too clean not to have
been done by someone thoroughly familiar with the
bank, but there was no conclusive evidence as to who
had done it. Years of litigation and irreversible personal
damage were followed by the confession, twenty-one
years after the robbery, of a convict in a New York
State prison. He was one of three professional burglars
who had arrived in Nantucket harbor on a sloop, done
the job, and left unnoticed at daybreak. No
Nantucketer had touched the money.

William Coffin was a director of the bank, and one
of those most active in promoting its establishment.
He was a respected, though controversial, figure in the
community. Many of the deals that originated in his
wig shop in town caused tongue-clickings and general
disapproval, but Coffin was a shrewd investor who had
shown himself capable of making money, and was fast
becoming a local political force to be reckoned with.
He was in his thirties when he became involved with
the bank, and had already been postmaster as well as
wig-maker. Intelligent, ambitious, Machiavellian by
nature, he was more successful than popular.

Whatever his reputation had been prior to the
robbery, it was certainly not improved by his
indictment before the Suffolk County Supreme Court
in 1797. Families had been pulled apart by anger and
suspicion over the theft, and William Coffin was later
to sue and actually beat up his distant cousin, Micajah
Coffin. A local religious pamphlet published in 1807
declared that the inhabitants of Nantucket " . . . no
longer live together like a family of brothers . . . They
hate and revile and persecute each other . . . It is
hoped that when the present generation, with their
prejudices and rancour shall have passed off the stage,

The iron railing on the front is the one that was on the steps of the Nantucket Bank when it was robbed in 1795.

the generation which succeeds will be restored to the sincerity, the good faith, the unsuspecting candour and the brotherly affection of former times . . ." In his own pamphlet, written shortly after the robbery, William Coffin claimed that he had been victimized by "chicanery," "phrenzy," and "moon-struck madness." He died a bitter man.

Coffin's house is a two-and-a-half-story, Federal-style building. The iron railing on the front is the one that was on the steps of the Nantucket Bank when it was robbed in 1795. The house is formal and prepossessing; one can easily imagine it standing at the head of Main Street.

Peter Benchley, best identified as author of the book *Jaws,* spent a summer alone in the house in the late '60s. At the time, it was owned by Marjorie Mills. The author had a strange experience that he says is clear to this day. He was in the house alone, and woke up from an afternoon nap in one of the bedrooms to see a fire burning in the fireplace and an old man sitting in front of the fire in a rocking chair, rocking gently. He had long hair and was dressed in eighteenth-century clothing. By the time Peter was fully awake, the man had vanished. There was no fire, and the chair was still. Benchley is convinced that what he saw was not a dream.

Marjorie Mills, who had loaned him the house as a summer workplace, was not surprised by his experience. She said that she had reason to believe the house had ghosts, but the details of her story have been lost, and she is no longer alive to recount the tale.

In 1970, Mr. and Mrs. John Tanner bought the house. Mrs. Tanner, who has since passed away, said in 1979 that it had been a peaceful house with the exception of a few inexplicable happenings.

In early spring, just after they had moved in, Mrs. Tanner was cleaning in the kitchen when she heard a crash from the library next door. She ran into the room and found that all the books from the middle shelf of a small standing bookcase were on the floor. The bookcase, enclosed on three sides, has sturdy wooden shelves that lift out of adjustable metal brackets. She knelt down and examined the middle shelf, which was still securely in place. The case would have to have been tipped forward in order for those books to fall, which would have emptied at least the top shelf too. Alternatively, someone would have had to reach in with a strong arm to sweep all the books off the middle shelf. A friend later suggested that she should have looked at the books themselves for an answer to their odd behavior, but a surprised Mrs. Tanner simply reshelved them and went back to the kitchen. She doesn't remember what the specific titles were, for they were in the house when the Tanners bought it, and have since been sold.

Several years later, Mrs. Tanner woke up at 4:00 A.M. to a loud whirring noise. She said it sounded exactly like a city streetcleaner's truck. She put on her bathrobe and went downstairs, only to find the empty electric blender in the kitchen buzzing away at high speed. The machine was a new and expensive one that had been used only two or three times. Mrs. Tanner was fascinated, for the appropriate push-button controls were indeed down. She wondered if a short-circuit or electrical surge could have turned it on and pulled in the buttons. That, however, seemed doubtful, and the Tanners began to joke about a resident ghost.

A third occurrence was even more puzzling. The
guest bedroom upstairs had twin four-poster beds with
detachable urn-shaped knobs on the tops. The knobs
were hand-turned and distinctive in shape. Mrs.
Tanner was cleaning the attic one day, and came
across a familiar-looking knob tucked away in a box of
buttons, screws, and household extras. She brought it
downstairs, and to her amazement found that it was
one of the eight knobs to the beds. She had no idea
how long the knob to the bedpost had been missing,
for the guest room had been closed up for several
months.

The Tanners' ghost experiences might be passed
off as having some natural explanation. Many residents
in town, however, will mention the house on Union
Street when asked about Nantucket ghosts. It seems
that generations of owners have murmured, *sotto voce*,
to neighbors and friends about goings-on in the house.
The building has a reputation for being slightly out of
the ordinary. But then, its original owner was no
ordinary man.

MERMAID

"I'll tell you about something that happened to me about three years ago in the Whaling Museum. I don't want you to use my name.

I'm sure I'd think it was laughable if it hadn't been me.

"My sister was on-island for a visit. It was a warmish spring day, and I suggested that we walk over to the Whaling Museum. We had both been there dozens of times before, but belonging as we do to an old Nantucket family, we have always been interested in the island's history. Well, we looked at the whaling gear and the big whale skeleton, and went through most of the museum. As we were just about ready to go, I was standing alone in a room of portraits, just looking around. My sister was out in the hall. Suddenly, I was aware of being stared at. Turning around, I looked right at the portrait of a pleasant-faced young man. He had regular features, nothing you might call distinctive. Now this sounds weird, but I was absolutely sure that I knew him – not recognized him, but *knew* him. The sensation was crystal clear. I hadn't the tiniest doubt that he and I were intimate friends, and had been for a long time, and the feeling was so overwhelming that I could only keep thinking, 'I *know* you! I *know* you!' It was as if he were my long-lost husband, but also as if it were happening to someone other than me. I'm a happily married woman, and this kind of thing is hardly in character. I was transfixed, absolutely absorbed, and that was part of what was so scary. I was held by a magnetism of some kind that was so strong I couldn't move. It wasn't that I was objectively interested in him, or thought I saw a family resemblance of some kind. It was rather that he had an iron grip on me.

"The next thing I knew, my sister had me by the arm and was pulling me out of the room, shaking me and asking what was wrong. She'd been standing in the doorway calling my name, and then watching me stare as if in a trance at this portrait. Even when we were out in the sunlight, I just wanted to get back and *see* that man, and kind of *be* with him. In all my previous visits to the museum, I don't remember ever having glanced twice at that portrait before.

"My sister was so unnerved by the way I had acted that I became scared, too, and went to my minister. He told me a story that really did me in. Now, before we get into what he told me, let me mention one thing. Ever since I was a child, I've had a recurrent 'memory,' I guess you'd call it, that pops into my mind from time to time. It's not a dream; it drifts across my thoughts when I'm fully awake. I've wondered from the time I was little where it came from and what it meant. It goes like this: I remember being in pitch blackness and having an excruciating pain in my side as I swim back and forth, back and forth, in black water. I also remember phosphorescence around me, the kind you see in the ocean on a dark night. I always thought it was peculiar, and I used to tell myself that maybe it was a memory of being inside the womb or something. I had told my husband about it, but no one else.

"When I went to see my minister after that experience in the museum, he said, trying to make me smile, 'Oh, my goodness! Don't you know the legend about that picture?' I said no, I didn't. He explained that the man in the painting had supposedly been in love with a mermaid, and that his wife was very jealous. She had a special silver-tipped harpoon made to kill this mermaid, and apparently hired someone who succeeded in carrying out the deed. Well, that, of course, made me think of that swimming memory I have. The whole thing just seemed too horribly coincidental, although I don't, of course, believe in mermaids.

"I haven't been back in the Whaling Museum since that day, although for months afterward I had a terrible craving to go back and see that painting. I'm a grown woman with grandchildren, but I would wake up in the middle of the night all upset, seeing that man's face as clear as day in my mind, and my husband would have to comfort me. I had trouble eating and sleeping. I was praying, all that time, that the man in that painting wouldn't bother me any more. The feeling of being magnetically drawn to that portrait to the point of obsession finally faded, thank God, but I'll never go back to the Whaling Museum as long as I live. I'm not that curious."

A VERY
LARGE CHIN

Jesse is seven years old. Her father and stepmother were invited to a party on India Street one July evening in 1981. Jesse came along with a bag of stuffed animals, crayons, and paper to keep herself amused.

She had exhausted her supplies by the time dinner was served. It was 9:00, and she was understandably cranky and tired. One of the guests suggested that she take an inventory of the first floor, noting down on her pad all the mirrors, all the candlesticks, all the brass doorknobs, and so forth. She thought that sounded interesting. The dinner guests could soon hear her busily counting away in the adjoining rooms and hallways.

A rambling, Federal-style structure, the house was built in 1831 by James Childs, the master carpenter who, with Christopher Capen, built the Three Bricks on Main Street. In 1972, the house was given to its present owners, Anne and Patrick Perkins, by an elderly woman named Emily Hunt. Mrs. Hunt's husband had died several years before she met the Perkinses.

Jesse had been quietly working on her project for a good half-hour when she came running into the dining room, shrieking that she had seen a man in the library. She was shaking, pale, and genuinely frightened. She blurted out that she had walked into the room and seen a man with a very large chin and a strange, dark-blue suit standing near a pair of rubber beach sandals that someone had left on the rug. He had tipped his hat to her, taken a couple of steps away from her, and vanished. She didn't mention the word ghost, and when questioned by her skeptical parents, simply reiterated how long his chin was. She said that he had looked at her with a "friendly, unscary face," and that he hadn't said anything.

None of the adults present took her experience too seriously, and she soon seemed to forget about it herself, settling down at her seat to have dessert with the grown-ups. In the weeks that followed, she didn't mention the experience to her parents again. The Perkinses had never seen or heard of a ghost in their house, and had also more or less forgotten Jesse's unlikely story until the following incident took place about a month later.

Jesse and her parents were visiting late one afternoon, and one of Mrs. Perkins's daughters brought out a line drawing that looked as though it had been done from a group photograph of a garden party. Clothing and people's hair styles placed the date of the drawing between 1940 and 1950. It had been found in the attic that day in the course of a search through old boxes for a missing item. The print was passed around as a curiosity, and Jesse, who was on the floor drawing a picture, took a casual look at it. Her face lit right up, and she said excitedly, "There he is! That's him!

There he is!" She pointed to a middle-aged man sitting with a woman underneath a shade umbrella. He did indeed have an extraordinarily prominent, square chin. He was identified, from a key on the back of the drawing, as Emily Hunt's husband, William. The Perkinses did some research on the man, hoping to find out more about him, but only came up with his death date, 1961, and the fact that he had committed suicide.

A LITTLE
GIRL

"**M**y son Jimmy suffered the most from this whole experience. He was just old enough to be really traumatized by what he had seen. He would never stay alone in the house after that, even during the day, and he would get jumpy and irritable when asked about her."

Joanne and Jim Shaw and their two children moved to the island from Rochester, New York, in 1972. Jim gave up his insurance business, and has worked since '72 as a fisherman. Joanne teaches dance classes and works at Even Keel, a clothing store on Main Street. The Shaws rented one of the old farmhouses in Polpis, on the north side of the island, from 1976 to 1980.

Joanne went on: "Jimmy was nine at the time. He and his sister Erin, who was six, had adjoining bedrooms upstairs; Jim and I slept on the first floor. Jimmy woke up one night to see a little girl standing in the dark by the side of his bed. He said, half asleep, 'What do you want, Erin?' When she didn't move or answer, it began to dawn on him that something was wrong. He jumped out of the other side of the bed and ran into Erin's room. She was fast asleep. He woke up his sister, and the two of them came thumping and shrieking downstairs and dove into bed with us. Jimmy was terrified, and had trouble sleeping for weeks afterward. In fact, we could never get him and Erin to sleep upstairs again. We eventually stopped trying, and set up a little bedroom for them down near ours.

"My husband and I thought Jimmy had probably had a bad nightmare, and we didn't pay much attention to his story. I did realize, however, that he was genuinely terrified by the memory of that little child.

"About a week later, all four of us were jammed into the double bed (Jim and I still hoping the kids would get over this and go back upstairs). It was a sticky, hot August night. All I could hear was the constant, piercing whine of mosquitoes. Each time one of us slapped, the others would get bounced, bumped, or woken up. I was in the middle. Finally I got up and stretched out on the living room couch. I was lying on my back, just drifting off, when I saw a little girl standing in the shadows on the other side of the room. She looked slightly taller than Erin. As I opened my eyes completely, she began to walk toward me. I remember that she was wearing a dark kerchief tied under her chin. Although I couldn't make out her facial features or the details of her body, I was aware that she was walking slowly, not drifting or floating. She had a long skirt or dress on. My first reaction to her approach was a strange one, and perhaps instinctive; I felt that she had mistaken me for her mother, and that she was coming over as if to give me a hug or nestle up to me. I felt a sudden rush of panic as she reached the end of the couch. I leaped up, exclaiming 'What in *heck* –!' As soon as I spoke, she vanished.

"I had never seen an apparition before, and would never have counted myself among the believers of such things; however, this child was real. She was no dream. The sight of her approaching me, her head hidden in that little kerchief, is still as vivid as can be – and it still gives me goosebumps.

"I was objectively curious about this little person, but I was also shaken. The idea that she might have mistaken me for her own mother was pathetic but, more than that, alarming; after all, my family and I had to go on living in the house. I guess I also felt vaguely guilty that I had jumped up from the couch. I had an unpleasant, lingering certainty that she had wanted something from me. I still wonder, at odd moments, what might have happened if I hadn't moved.

"I brought the kids' things downstairs the next day, and we converted a small room off the front hallway into a bedroom for them. I told my husband about having seen Emily, as we later named her, on the night it happened. I told my kids the next morning, and Jimmy was reassured to hear that I had also seen the little girl. I tried to present the experience in a matter-of-fact way. If we had to share the house with a ghost, I thought it was best that we try to be straightforward about it.

"I did look into the history of the house. It was built in the first quarter of the nineteenth century. I talked with some of the older Nantucketers in Polpis, but they didn't remember hearing of any strange incidents connected with the property. The little girl, of course, could conceivably have died many generations ago.

"A couple of weeks later, on a stormy, windy

night, Emily turned up again. Jim had set the alarm for 3 A.M. in order to go out fishing. Shortly before the alarm went off, we were awakened from a sound sleep by a howling just outside our bedroom window. It really didn't sound like a domestic dog; the tone was closer to that of a coyote. It was probably someone's stray, caught in the storm, but it sure was a desolate, eerie sound. Neither one of us could get back to sleep, and Jim got up to take his shower.

"He didn't tell me this at the time, not wanting to frighten me, but as soon as he opened our bedroom door, he could feel that there was someone out in the hallway between our room and the bathroom. I did notice that he stood in our open bedroom door for a minute or so before going down the hall. Faced with this sense of an unknown presence standing in front of him in the dark, he actually put his head down, stretched one arm out in front of him, and walked (or, rather, dove) down the dark hallway to the bathroom. He switched the light on, and looked back to find that the hall was empty. He took his shower and left the house.

"I was just dozing off again when I felt the bed go down on one side. Apparently, someone had sat down next to me. I was lying on my stomach, my arms tucked under me. I thought at first that it was one of the kids, but when no one spoke, my heart started beating faster. Before I could lift my head or look around, I felt someone sitting on my upper back – someone about the weight of a young child. I then felt – oh, God, this gives me the creeps! – a hand stroking the back of my head. I don't know whether it was five minutes or a few seconds, but it seemed to go on forever.

"I couldn't move. I don't know if you've ever had dreams where you're being pursued by something and your legs melt beneath you, but it was just that kind of feeling. I didn't seem to have any muscles. Pinned under this unseen weight, I just lay there feeling the soft, intermittent stroking on the back of my head. Then the adrenalin began to flow, and gathering all my strength I flung myself out of bed, half falling on the floor. I remember shrieking, 'Get out of here! Get out of here!'

"Needless to say, I was up the rest of the morning. When Jim got in later in the day, and I told him, shakily, what had happened, he said 'Oh, yes, she was out in the hallway when I got up.' I could have killed him for not telling me before he left the house!

"There were times when I would walk into my bedroom during the day and feel that she was sitting on a caned chair in the corner by one of the windows. I couldn't see anything, but I would look over there, and then I would hear a rustle from the chair seat, as if someone had just stood up. This would be followed by sequential creaking of the floor boards, as if she were walking around the edge of the room. The creaking always followed the same route, moving around by the wall, in front of my dresser, and out the door. It was as if I had disturbed her, and she got up and left the room.

"The following winter we went to Florida for a couple of weeks. I packed everything away and closed up the house. When we got home, I opened the front door to find hundreds of dead black flies in the foyer. They were great big horse flies, the kind you don't usually see inside in the winter. They were so thick underfoot that I swept up a big dustpan-full of them.

What a horrible welcome! Even worse, when I went to put the kids to bed, I turned back their covers and found that both of their beds were filled with the same kind of large dead flies. They were under the covers, as if someone had turned back each bed, thrown the flies in on the bottom sheet, and then made the beds up again.

"Although Jimmy only saw Emily that one night, he definitely had a harder time dealing with the idea of her apparent existence than the rest of us did. As long as we lived in that house, he was afraid of being alone, couldn't sleep, and worried that he would see her again. I must admit that my initial feeling of sympathy for the little girl changed pretty rapidly to one of apprehension and, after that experience in the bedroom, simple horror. The sight of her, the feeling of being pinned on my bed and having someone touching the back of my head, the creaking sounds, the black flies – living with that unknown child is something I'll never forget."

SIXTEEN
MEN

"Grace and I were alone in the house, sleeping in adjoining bedrooms. We had spent the evening at home, had two glasses of wine apiece with dinner, and had taken nothing alcoholic since then. Grace got up at 2:15 A.M. for an extra blanket, and happened to look out the window. There were several people outside. She came into my room and woke me up."

This incident occurred in 1977, on the Friday before Halloween. Marcia Hart, who now lives on Nantucket, was then a student at Brown University. She had come to the island for the weekend to visit her friend Grace Patterson; it was Grace's first winter on Nantucket, and she was renting a new house on the outskirts of town. The two young women had become friends during a summer of waitressing together. Marcia continued:

"We left the lights out, and stood by the window in Grace's bedroom. It was below freezing, and there was plenty of starlight but no moon. The back yard had no grass or trees, for it had only recently been cleared. It consisted of about fifty square yards of mounded dirt and sand, which ended at the back of the Chicken Box bar. On the left was an unpaved parking lot, and on the right a new house. Sure enough, about ten feet from the back of the bar, I could see six men in white pants. Their shirts were dark, and there was not enough light to see their features clearly. They didn't appear to be wearing bulky winter clothing. They were lifting and tugging a large, heavy object about the size and shape of a shipping crate, or of a refrigerator laid on its side. Occasionally one or another of them would straighten up and stop for rest. There was no wind, and while we could hear low voices, we couldn't make out any words. Now and then we could hear the scrabble of loose pebbles as a boot scraped on the frozen ground.

"I called the police. Soon we could hear the patrol car coming, and as the headlights swept across the yard, the men got down on all fours and rolled into the deep, irregular troughs between the heaps of dirt. Two patrolmen climbed out and, standing next to their car, beamed their flashlights back and forth. Nothing to be seen. The rear of the building was thrown into shadow by the headlights, and the large object the men had been trying to move was not visible. It was a bitterly cold night, so without having left the side of their car, after a quick look around, the patrolmen climbed back in and drove away.

"We saw the men crawl up out of the ditches as the taillights disappeared down the street. They went on with their work as more of them appeared from the front side of the building; soon a dozen men were taking turns at moving the large rectangular object.

"Four men were hoisted up onto the roof of the

building. We could see first one and then another crouching in silhouette on the ridge, apparently talking to the men below. A figure was sitting in the driver's seat of my VW bug, which I had left unlocked. He was bobbing up and down as if he were working on something down near the floor. Feet crossed and recrossed the line of light under the back door of the bar; it seemed that the men had gotten inside the building.

"Several hours went by as we pointed out different figures to each other and tried to keep track of how many there were. The men moved lightly, with rapid, animated motions, and none of them looked very tall. We were tense, and careful not to let them see us. I remember feeling strangely lucid. Looking back, I'm puzzled and surprised – and troubled – that we didn't immediately call the police again. After all, we were sitting by, glued to the window, whispering to each other while we watched a bunch of men robbing a bar. That's not exactly a normal reaction, and not the kind of thing either of us would do. It makes me wonder if those men had some sort of numbing effect on us. I suppose we were waiting until the sky lightened and we could see what the men were doing, although that now seems like an inadequate explanation.

"Shortly after 4:30, we counted sixteen men behind the Chicken Box. The large object had been moved approximately twenty feet along the back of the building. The figures seemed to be taking turns at different activities: some climbed up on the roof, others moved this object, still others just walked back and forth. We watched until dawn. As the sky began to lighten, it became apparent to us both that the figures were fading. They continued with their activities, but were becoming increasingly difficult to see. We were appalled. I felt suddenly nauseous, and Grace just kept saying, 'Oh, my God! This is ridiculous!' over and over. By the time the first real flush of pink hit the sky, the yard was empty."

Neither Marcia nor Grace had ever seen an apparition or ghost before that night, nor have they since. Marcia's car battery was dead the following morning, but that was the only possible physical trace that the men had left behind. The rectangular object they had been struggling with had disappeared with them. Nathaniel Benchley, on hearing this story, remarked that the area was reputed to have been a connection point for rumrunners during Prohibition. The Chicken Box, a one-story frame building, was built in the 1950s, and is now a popular bar that stays open all year.

A SHAKER
ROCKER

"**M**y wife and I are antique dealers, and bought our house on Union Street in September of 1967. We're from Connecticut, and had opened a small branch of our mainland business on one of the wharves here the previous summer. We fell in love with the island, and began looking for a place to live at the end of the season. Once we set foot in the house, we knew immediately that it had to be ours. It all happened very quickly. We moved in, and began stripping off all kinds of trim and overlay. The floors were covered with linoleum, the fireplaces were blocked up, the lights, or small fire windows over the doors, were painted over. We unmasked the house, room by room, doing most of the restoration work ourselves.

"I looked into the history of the house and found that it had been built by Captain Joseph West in 1802. When his wife, Mary, died in 1816, West sold the house to Captain Obed Cathcart for $1,300. Cathcart lived in the house with his wife, Sally McCleave, until his death in 1861. They had no children, and the house then passed to Cathcart's niece, Nancy M. Coffin, who in turn willed it to her husband, Alfred M. Coffin. Alfred Coffin sold it to the Home for Aged People in Winchester in 1895, and Mary J. Gifford Smith bought it from them in the same year. It was sold in 1917 to Mr. and Mrs. William Hall, who owned the house until 1954, when they sold it to Arthur and Jessie Stetson. We bought it from the Stetsons, making a total of only seven families in the house over the past 181 years.

"One January day in '68 we were working on the large fireplace in the keeping room. There was a loose board bulging out above the fireplace, and I couldn't make it lay flat. This section had been plastered over and wallpapered. I tapped it, and it sounded hollow. We scraped and peeled and eventually pried up the board. Inside was a small cupboard with shallow shelves, the type of storage area known as a parson's cupboard. It had been sealed, from the looks of the wall, for at least a century. A small section of the shelving had dried out and disintegrated, and as we dug deeper we found several small utilitarian objects that had fallen down between the shelving and the wall: an ivory comb, a bottle, a pin cushion, and a flint, all dating back to the first half of the nineteenth century. They were personal, everyday things that had probably gotten pushed into the corner of the cupboard and then fallen through the rotted area in the shelving. We put all of these little objects on the top of a sea chest sitting in the room, and left them out that night when we went to bed.

"It was a clear, moonlit winter night. My wife, Kay, and I were sleeping on a mattress in the bedroom on one side of the keeping room, and our one-year-old son was sleeping in the room on the other side. My wife woke me up at about one o'clock and asked if I would go check on our son, who was fussing a bit. I got up and started through the door of the keeping room. We had no curtains, and the room was bright in the moonlight, filled with that lovely gray-blue tone that comes from a full moon in a clear sky. Suddenly, I froze. A little Shaker rocking chair sitting a few feet from the fireplace was moving as if someone had just been rocking and then had stood up. You know, one – two – three, each rock smaller than the last one. As I peered into the room, trying to see if anyone was there, I had the definite feeling that I had startled someone rocking in the chair, and that the person had jumped up and hurried to the far corner of the room where a closet door stood open in the shadows. I stood still for, I guess, a couple of minutes, looking into the corner to see if I could make out anything resembling a figure. I couldn't, but I just knew there was a person, or perhaps I should say a presence, hiding from me in the dark. I was shaken, and since our son had quieted down, I went back to bed and told Kay what had happened. She got up and went to the doorway. The chair had stopped moving, but to my surprise she, too, had a clear impression that someone was standing in the corner of the room. It wasn't threatening or evil, but it was a little scary. We didn't walk over to the corner or shine a light into the room out of some feeling, I suppose, that we had already disturbed that presence, whatever it was, and that we should leave well enough alone. I couldn't help wondering if our discovery of the objects in the parson's cupboard had anything to do with this weird experience.

"As we worked on the house, we began to come

across the name Obed Cathcart in all sorts of odd places. Late one afternoon I was busy with something downstairs and felt a sudden urge to go up to the attic, which was empty at the time. I got a flashlight, went up, and found myself crawling into a little cranny in the eaves. Nailed to the wall were several pieces of what looked like an old hatbox, deep in a corner where there would ordinarily be no reason even to look. I pulled them off the wall, and on the cover of the hatbox was written in bold lettering, 'Captain Obed Cathcart.'

"This business of feeling impelled to look in a certain place and then finding his name happened a number of times. It was as if I were suddenly directed by a firm, friendly hand toward a specific spot. I remember working one day in my son's room, where we had taken up the linoleum. I noticed a seam in the floor, and found myself digging down under the board. I popped it up, and sure enough, written on a long strip of paper were the words 'Captain Obed Cathcart.' He had buried his name all over the house; it was as if I were satisfying some old urge of his by uncovering it.

"I did some research on the man and found that he had made several whaling voyages to the Pacific between 1826 and 1838 on the *Elizabeth Starbuck* and the *James Loper* out of Nantucket, and on the *Victory* and the *Young Phoenix* out of New Bedford. He left Nantucket again in 1850 as captain of the *Ontario*. The ship was condemned at Tahiti, and its seven-hundred-barrel cargo of sperm oil was shipped to England.

"Obed bought the house when he was twenty-eight, three years after he and his wife, Sally, were married. He lived there for the remaining forty-four years of his life, and died a poor man. He left five

A little Shaker rocking chair sitting a few feet from the fireplace was moving as if someone had just been rocking and then had stood up.

dollars apiece to his brothers, Seth and David. To his
niece, Nancy Coffin, he willed the house; in the
Probate Court inventory, he left her the furniture 'in
Front chamber and basement,' appraised at $62.00; six
large silver spoons and eighteen small ones, worth
$18.00; and one rocking chair, worth $3.00.

"It seems strange that a whaling captain who had
made so many trips should die with so little to his
name. And he was apparently a good man. I have a
clipping about a rescue he made from the *James Loper*
in 1839. A Japanese junk, the *Chôja Maru,* was
wrecked in January of that year and had been drifting
for six months when it was sighted by Cathcart. He
took the seven surviving crew members to Hawaii,
where a certain Dr. Baldwin wrote, 'It is due to the
kindness and generosity of Captain C., generosity often
met with among seafaring men, . . . that not only were
these sufferers provided with food and necessary
clothing but . . . were landed here, with all the
moveable property they had saved, including a
considerable amount of money . . . all which, on their
escaping the wreck, was put into the care of Capt. C.,
but none was reserved by way of compensation.' I have
a feeling that he was a modest man, and probably a
Quaker, who just never made it big.

"My wife and I came to accept, early on, the
presence of a benevolent personality in the house. It's
a wonderful house, and we've never been
uncomfortable in it, but we definitely were sharing it in
those early years. And there were times when Kay or I
would see someone just flitting around the edge of a
doorway, crossing a passageway, or disappearing
around a corner when we knew there was no one
there. We would catch a fleeting, peripheral glimpse of

a back or of a piece of clothing. I remember one time when I was just starting up the stairs and saw a woman in a dress stepping quickly through the hall into the next room. I didn't think anything of it, assuming it was Kay, and went up the stairs and into the room across the way. I said something to Kay, and when I got no answer, I looked upstairs and then down only to find that she wasn't even in the house.

"That little Shaker rocker has been something of an enigma too. As a rule, my memory about where and when I acquire antiques is excellent; as you know, we're dealers, and we do a brisk business in Nantucket pieces out of our shop on North Water Street. But I can't, for the life of me, remember where that rocker came from. At some point shortly after we moved in I sold it, but I can't remember whom I sold it to, either. And I don't seem to have any sales slips on it; it's almost as though I have a mental block about that little chair. At any rate, a woman on Quince Street called me a few years ago and said she had a little Shaker rocker she wanted to get rid of. She didn't tell me why; she just said she wanted it out. I went over to pick it up, and sure enough, there was our little chair. We have it back at the house now, and ever since it has been back we've had no disturbances of any kind.

"I'll have to look that woman up and ask her why she wanted to get rid of it."

CHRISTMAS MUSIC

Peter Guarino and Paul Willer bought 25 Orange Street in 1971. Peter recently related the following account.

"Paul and I came from Manhattan to Nantucket for a weekend in 1969, and it seemed like paradise. Although we're New Yorkers through and through, we'd had it with the city; we were both just exhausted from years of struggling with urban living, and we looked at each other and said, 'Let's do it. Let's sell it all and move to Nantucket.'

"We decided to look for a guest house. It took us two years of flying back and forth from the city before we found 25 Orange. The minute we set foot in it, we knew it was just right. We've named it The House of Orange.

"We had a strange but very pleasant recurring experience our first four years in the house. At midnight every Christmas Eve, we would hear organ music coming from the third floor. It lasted for about ten minutes. It wasn't any Christmas music that we recognized, but it was beautiful. When we went up there we could hear it more clearly, but we couldn't pinpoint the spot that it was coming from. Needless to say, there was no organ there.

"The third floor had been full of boxes of sheet music when we moved in. With a little research, I found out that a minister of St. Paul's Episcopal Church, a Mr. Snelling, had lived in the house for many years. He had used the third floor as his study, and apparently had an organ up there. His widow left the house to the church, and since the church was unable to use it, the house stood empty for four years before it changed hands.

"As we see it, Mr. Snelling was making up for those years when the house had no music on Christmas Eve."

THE HOUSE
THAT KILLED
MY FATHER

"The house was utterly luxurious. It had every amenity one could want: marble showers, tiled floors, two ovens, lots of space, a terrific location. And yet, of all the houses Carol and I have lived in, that was the only one we really didn't like."

Bob Miller was standing, hammer in hand, in the warm April sunshine. To the left of his head swung a sign lettered "Robert J. Miller, Hairdressers, Men and Women." Sounds of hammers and the buzz of a chain saw came from inside the building. Bob and his wife, Carol, were helping carpenters with preseason alterations in their store on Washington Street. Bob went on:

"Carol and I bought the house in 1976. It's on the southeast end of the island, and was started in 1964 by a man named William Cammon Bantry. He died suddenly, before the house was finished, and we bought the property from his widow. It was our first home on Nantucket, and we were all ready to love it. Our kids were excited about moving here, and we looked forward to working on the place.

"From the very first, though, the house felt funny. For instance, although it was soundly built, there were times when you were inside, sitting on a chair where no draft would seem possible, and you'd have the feeling of air moving around you, almost of unnatural breezes. We had some old English chairs with high upholstered backs and wings – chairs designed to protect one from drafts. Even sitting in those chairs, I would still feel as if something were blowing on me. We never could get the house cozy and warm in the winter.

"The fireplace in the den smoked terribly. We had a mason come to inspect the chimney more than once; he couldn't find any reason for its not drawing properly. I always blamed it on some sort of adverse air circulation in the building, but actually that didn't make much sense. We finally just gave up on fires.

"I remember that the house also had an unpleasant smell, one that seemed to come and go. It sounds funny now, but it was really quite awful. At first we thought that an animal had died under the building or in the walls. The smell resembled that of a dead dog or rotten onions. I finally went down to check the crawlspace under the house, but I didn't find anything. We discovered that the smell would come and just as suddenly go, on its own.

"The only room where we all felt comfortable was a large, enclosed back sunporch, a porch that we discovered was a later addition to the original plan of the house. We tended to gravitate toward that porch; we even put our Christmas tree out there, if you can believe it. I remember Carol saying to me that the living room was too dark for Christmas.

"The unpleasant feeling in the house affected us all, although we were reluctant at first to admit it. We're an easygoing family, but while we were living in that house little things seemed to get us irritated at each other all the time. I'm convinced, looking back on it, that something about the building itself put a strain on us all. In rational terms, there was absolutely nothing wrong: we adored Nantucket, the house itself was beautiful, the kids were doing well, our business was underway, we had no financial problems. And yet we found ourselves constantly tired and grumpy and nervous.

"It all came to a head with some unexpected visitors. I was working on the accounts, I think, when Carol and I heard some people knocking at the back door. I remember suddenly feeling that I didn't want to know who it was. I kept my head down and said to Carol, 'I don't want to see them. I really don't. I can't. I'm not going to answer it.' She gave me a strange look and went to see who it was. Normally, I enjoy people and am a pretty conversational, open type, but I didn't look up, even when I heard Carol showing these visitors around the house. When they left, she came in, looking upset, and told me that one of them was the daughter of the man who built the house. The woman had said to Carol that she and her husband had made a special trip to Nantucket just to see 'the house that killed my father.'

"I felt numb when I heard that. It sounds overly dramatic, but I really felt numb. I think those words brought to the surface an unspoken fear that there was something bad in the house, something horrible that we had been living with. And it scared me that I had acted so strangely; I hadn't, for some reason, wanted to meet Mr. Bantry's daughter. That's not like me. It's almost as if I didn't want to hear what she was going to say. That's when Carol and I began to take our feelings about the house seriously.

"Unable to forget those words, I asked around and found out that William Bantry had encountered a number of difficulties in building the house. He remarried at the time the house was under construction, and his new wife was not crazy about Nantucket. She made change after change in the plans as the building was going up. It was started in one direction, pulled down, and started in another. And then Mr. Bantry died quite unexpectedly of a heart attack.

"All of this is certainly not to say that Mr. Bantry had anything to do with the unpleasant feeling in the house. I have no idea why the place had a bad aura to it, but as soon as we sold it and moved to town in '78, we felt a tremendous relief. Something in that house had a pernicious effect on us all."

Pepper Frazier, a real estate broker, and his wife, Libby, bought the house from the Millers. The Fraziers have two sons: Pepper, who was three years old when they moved in, and Dalton, who was three months. The Millers hadn't said anything to the Fraziers concerning their bad feelings about the house. Libby Frazier tells the following story.

"There was something very wrong with that place. From the time we first settled in, strange things kept happening to Dalton. When he was really tiny, I would sit him up on the floor, turn around to do something, and then hear the clunk of his little head on the wood. It was awful. I couldn't figure it out, for he wasn't that unsteady. It was as if someone had given him a good push. This happened many times when his brother was nowhere near him.

"There were also times over the next couple of years when he would be lying quietly in his crib and would suddenly scream out, as if he'd been pinched or startled. One morning he had a really bad scratch on his face. His father and I were beginning to feel a bit panicky.

"As you can imagine, we were reluctant to think that there could be anything in the house that was tormenting Dalton, knowing how foolish that sounded, but the poor little boy had one accident after another. Many of them happened for no plausible reason. He isn't an uncoordinated child, and it really began to appear as though someone invisible was doing things to him. He hated being alone in his bedroom. He would fall repeatedly and get all sorts of lumps, bruises, and scratches. He even hit his head so badly once that he began to hemorrhage internally. We rushed him to Massachusetts General, where they operated on him immediately. He's fine now, but looking back on it, I have to think that some force or spirit in the house took a violent dislike to the baby and was really out to hurt him.

"His father and I both saw a little figure that wasn't either one of our boys. We'd had a ghost in our house in Marblehead, so the idea of seeing one didn't scare us too much, but there was something utterly chilling about the ghost of a small child in this new house, a ghost about the same size and age as our boys. My husband saw him first. He looked outside one winter day and saw a towhead run quickly by under the window. From what we saw of the top of his head, the child looked just like Dalton. It wasn't. The kids were nowhere near, and we had no neighbors with small children.

"I saw a little figure one day during the summer. I had been out doing errands, and just after I walked in the door a child ran by at the other end of the house. I called out, 'Hi, everybody. I'm home!' There was no answer. I looked around and realized that the boys and my husband were still at the beach. That scared me, for I was absolutely certain I had seen a little person scampering by in the house. It wasn't a peripheral flicker of something solid; it was definitely a child.

"Ever since we moved into town, Dalton has been fine. The accident-after-accident business stopped when we settled into our new house. I suppose that all of the things that happened could have had rational explanations, but I just know, perhaps intuitively, that they didn't. When I think back on how that house felt, what happened to Dalton in it, and the little child my husband and I both saw, I just know there was something very wrong."

BRUSHING
MY CHEEK

"I told a few people about this experience back when it was going on, and they made fun of me. Know what I mean? Told me I was crazy. I kept quiet about it after that."

Mr. and Mrs. David Greenberg were, for many years, the proprietors of a family restaurant on Nantucket, and are well-loved citizens of the island. Their house, built in 1847, is in the center of town.

Mr. Greenberg leaned over, clicked off the evening news, and settled back in his chair.

"Let's see now. I guess it would have been 1952 or 1953. I was awakened in the night several times during that two-year period by the feeling of someone brushing a hand softly across my cheek, just like this, lightly stroking the side of my face. It was pleasant, gentle. I would open my eyes and see a vague form of a woman drifting across our room near the foot of the bed. There's a word for it, can't think what, like protoplasm — something that moves and changes shape. She was filmy, know what I mean? She didn't walk; she moved smoothly. She wore a long, loose gown. She wasn't solid enough for me to make out her features or her expression. And – now this is peculiar – she never made me nervous. I was startled, but not nervous. I knew, without thinking, that she was a kind person. Don't know why. Just sensed it. By the time I was awake enough to nudge my wife, there was nothing there."

Mrs. Greenberg put down her needlework. "I always believed my husband, although I never actually saw her. He and I didn't pay much attention to these nighttime visitations; we were busy, and we just took it in stride. We never told our children about it, not seeing any reason to scare them with it, and not knowing quite what to make of it ourselves.

"One Thanksgiving, when our daughter Mary was five or six, she told me that a strange lady had stood by her bed during the night.

"'Oh?' I said, 'And what was she like, dear?'

"'She was a nice lady, Mommy.' Those were her first words. She went on to tell me that the woman had a long neck, and was wearing a funny, floor-length dress with a high collar. She explained that the figure looked just like one of the Pilgrims. Mary wasn't at all scared. In fact, she was emphatic about liking this woman. The 'nice lady' stood by her bed, smiled down at her, and walked out of her bedroom and into ours. Mary watched her go and then rolled over and apparently went right back to sleep."

Mr. Greenberg picked up the story. "I saw the woman that same night. I woke to the familiar sensation of a soft stroking on the side of my face, but this time, when I opened my eyes, she was standing right by the side of the bed, looking down at me. She was much more distinct than before, almost solid, and

I remember her as having a kind expression, although I couldn't see her features clearly. Her neck *was* very long, and bent strangely to the side, know what I mean? I don't know why it didn't spook me. I remember wondering, at the time, if her neck were bent that way because she had been hanged. Maybe she was slightly deformed. Who knows? After a few moments, she turned away and walked through the closed door of our closet and disappeared.

"We never saw her again."

EXPECTING THE INEXPLICABLE

The house is a multilayered structure. Over the past century and a half, the original building has been added on to many times. It is hard to tell what came after what, for some of the additions were once freestanding houses. While the clapboard exterior has an organized appearance, the interior structure is confusing in a pleasant way: floor planking changes direction and tone, ceilings rise and sink, baseboards meet up with each other with the awkward amiability of distant cousins.

Mr. and Mrs. Allan Shriver bought the house in 1966. When interviewed in 1980, they described the variety of things that happened there as "fantastic." During their first summer in the house, the family returned from the beach late one July afternoon. Walking with bare feet across the dining room to the kitchen, Mrs. Shriver stepped on a small wet spot on the rug. She doubled back to take a look. The ceiling wasn't leaking, and nothing had been spilled or overturned. Oddly enough, the pad underneath the rug was bone-dry. It didn't seem possible.

The spot got bigger and bigger over the next few days, spreading imperceptibly from the size of a dinner plate to a circle over three feet in diameter. Sopping didn't help. Mrs. Shriver called the plumber. He came to the house but was also unable to figure out where the spot came from. This went on for about a month. They simply tromped around or across the huge wet spot, for there wasn't much they could do. One morning it disappeared as suddenly as it had come, leaving no odor, residue, or stain.

Two months later, in September, the Shrivers' son Christopher came for a visit. Christopher went out with some friends one evening, and his parents had a dinner engagement. Mrs. Shriver had made a point of asking Christopher not to bring friends back to the house late that night.

The Shrivers left the dinner party and went to bed early. Mrs. Shriver wasn't feeling well, and hadn't had anything to drink for at least forty-eight hours. (She emphasizes this detail, knowing that skeptics love to connect ghosts with dinner wine.) Lying in bed, she heard the clock strike twelve, followed by the sounds of Christopher and his friends coming in. Subdued giggling, talking, and the clinking of ice in glasses drifted up the stairs. She was irritated, but decided to wait until the following morning to speak to him about it. She heard the group babbling away for a good hour; then the clock struck one. When Christopher tiptoed up the stairs at about quarter past one, she called him into her room. She whispered a fierce "Now look, dear —" from the bed, and he simply stood in the doorway, shrugged, turned on his heel, and marched down the hall to his room. He slammed the door.

Over breakfast the next morning she asked him why he had been so inconsiderate. Christopher was surprised. He told her that he hadn't come home until 3:30, and had been alone and gone right to bed. There was, indeed, no evidence of a late party downstairs. She found it hard to believe. She knew what she had heard, and he knew what he had done; they argued back and forth. The incident was so odd that Christopher brought his friends over to vouch for him. He was evidently telling the truth, for he had been at a neighbor's house until after 3:00 A.M. In thinking over the experience, Mrs. Shriver remembered that in the darkness she had seen the outline of his figure standing in the doorway, but had been unable to see his face. As crazy as it seemed, the sounds she heard and the figure she saw evidently had nothing to do with Christopher. It was at this point that the family began to joke, incredulously, about a resident ghost.

Several weeks after this happened, the Shrivers were sitting downstairs alone when they heard someone pacing back and forth in their bedroom. An even, deliberate step traversed the length of the room, paused, and walked back. It sounded like the firm, leather-soled step of a man, and went on for a good ten or fifteen minutes. The pacing occurred frequently over the next three years, and the Shrivers soon paid no more attention to it than they might have to a ticking clock or a squeaking door. It was never heard when anyone was upstairs, nor did it happen at any special time of day or in any particular weather.

At times, when they were in their bedroom, they heard a sharp, staccato rapping on the door. Mr. Shriver described it as an imperative "Goddammit, I want to talk to you" type of knocking, loud enough to awaken both of them from a sound sleep. Unlike the pacing, which had the self-absorbed rhythm of someone brooding, the rapping was angry and urgent. When he got out of bed and opened the door, there was never anyone there.

In 1966 and 1967, when they were frequently hearing the footsteps and the rapping, the Shrivers lived alone in the house. Around this time they also had a problem with slamming doors, which would clap shut with a ferocious bang on still nights when no draft could be detected.

Most of these abnormal goings-on stopped after several years. Whatever was in the house seemed to quiet down. Then, one May, they had what must be one of the most generous and imaginative poltergeist visitations on record.

The Shrivers have a miniature nineteenth-century desk in their living room. About two feet high, it was probably a furniture-maker's showroom model. When Mrs. Shriver bought it, back in the late '50s in New York, one of its five drawers was missing an ivory pull. The knobs are the size of almonds and have a distinctive yellow patina that can only come from age and wear. Each knob is ringed with tiny carved bands. The Shrivers didn't attempt to replace the missing pull.

When opening up the house recently, the Shrivers found the French doors dividing the living room from the porch stuck closed. The doors are about fifteen feet from the desk, and fasten with a vertical lock that slides into a small square hole in the floor. When they finally shot the rod up, they found an ivory pull jammed into the lock bed. The pull is indistinguishable from the other four on the desk, and is similarly worn with age. Surprisingly, it wasn't damaged or crushed.

The Shrivers have absolutely no idea where it came from, for the desk had been cleaned and polished many times over the years, and the missing knob had never turned up. The house had been empty all winter, and employees who were with them when they found it vouch for the fact that the Shrivers didn't invent the story. The fifth pull has been screwed into place on the desk drawer, where it sits today.

The house ghost, poltergeist, gift horse, or whatever it might be, apparently has a cultural bent, for over the years, original copies of the musical *No, No, Nanette* (Mr. Shriver is related to lyricist Otto Harbach) and two slim volumes of *The Kings and Queens of France* have disappeared and just as inexplicably reappeared several weeks later in their places on the library shelf. The employees have never shown interest in these books, and Mr. and Mrs. Shriver are quite sure that they weren't playing tricks on each other. Both had noted this strange situation at different times, and neither found it amusing.

The only phenomenon that has been a constant is the ringing telephone in the Shrivers' bedroom. Every night just after midnight, the bedside phone gives three feeble chirps. They are shorter than a normal ring, and Mrs. Shriver described them as the kind of quick, anemic "*brrt*" sound sometimes heard from a phone during a big electrical storm. When the receiver is picked up, a regular dial tone is heard. If someone is using the phone at the time the chirping usually occurs, it functions normally. They have contacted the phone company several times to find out whether crossed lines, electrical surges, or some other mechanical foul-up could be responsible. The answer seems to be no.

The house on Main Street was built by John Gardner in the 1830s. The land had originally belonged to his great-umpteenth grandfather, Richard Gardner, in 1673. After John Gardner repurchased the family land in the early nineteenth century, it was passed from generation to generation. Shortly after the house was built, as the story goes, two Gardner brothers brought a Chinese houseboy back from a voyage. His presence on the island was probably unusual enough for families to inquire about where he lived and whom he worked for. One day he simply disappeared. He had apparently overstepped his bounds with one of the Gardner sisters, whose brothers murdered the boy in a fit of rage. There are no papers to document the death, and the Gardner brothers were never brought to trial, but the story was recorded by several contemporaries. It was said that the murder took place upstairs, in what later became the Shrivers' bedroom.

A FLYING CANDLESTICK

The house was built in 1785 on Center Street and was restored and divided into five small apartments in the 1960s. Larry Vienneau and Malcolm Barreiros shared one of the ground-floor apartments during the winter season of 1977–78. Larry is a painter, printmaker and scrimshander; Malcolm was the chef at the India House for several years, and is now the *sous-chef* at the Second Story Restaurant.

The apartment was an ideal winter rental. It was cozy and warm, and was right in the middle of town. The combination of low, eighteenth-century ceilings, exposed beams, plastered walls, and original floorboards guaranteed that no surface was quite level and no line quite straight. The place seemed to toss and roll with a stubborn will of its own, and visitors were often thrown off balance in trying to navigate from room to room.

Malcolm had the smaller and darker of the bedrooms. Although freshly painted and scrubbed, the room had a sour, bitter smell to it when he arrived

there. It had not improved any by the time he moved
out. He tried leaving his window open for days on end,
dragging the furniture out, washing the walls and floor,
and even burning incense. The odor persisted.
Malcolm's old dog would stick his head into the room
when his master called him from inside, and then,
blinking apologetically, would turn and slink back into
the living room. Malcolm tried carrying him in and
setting him down. The dog would scramble for the
door, his tail between his legs. A cat stayed in the
apartment for several weeks that winter, and she never
willingly entered Malcolm's room either. When carried
in, she would squirm and scratch and leap for the door.

Larry and Malcolm had an old stereo in the living
room. Every so often, one of them would go to put on
a record and find that the air just above and around the
turntable was freezing cold. Anyone who happened to
be in the apartment could run a hand in and out of the
cold spot; it had definite boundaries, and could be felt
even when the rest of the apartment was a comfortable
65 to 70 degrees. Malcolm says he remembers one
morning when his girlfriend was staying for the
weekend, and the entire living room suddenly felt like
a walk-in freezer, but the thermostat registered a
normal 65 degrees.

One December afternoon Larry was alone in the
apartment, listening to the stereo while working on a
piece of scrimshaw in his bedroom. He went into the
living room to change a record and noticed that the
cold spot above the turntable was back again. He
didn't think much of it, crossed the room to the
cabinet where he kept his albums, and was just
bending over to pull one out when something very
heavy hit the wall near his head with a sharp crack. He

The combination of low, eighteenth-century ceilings, exposed beams, plastered walls, and original floorboards guaranteed that no surface was quite level and no line quite straight.

jumped up, his heart thudding. An oversized pewter candlestick that had come with the apartment was lying on the floor at his feet. The candlestick, which was kept on a table next to the stereo, had apparently flown diagonally across the room, a distance of about ten feet, and crashed next to Larry. It would have taken a strong arm to throw the candlestick that hard. Larry felt the hair rising on the back of his neck.

Malcolm arrived home ten minutes later, and when Larry told him what had happened, he laughed and just said, "Jesus, Larry, what's wrong? Long winter?" Going into the kitchen, Malcolm put the groceries down and started dinner. Larry was shaken, but he laughed too, and shrugged. Joining Malcolm in the kitchen, he picked up a towel to dry some of the dishes on the drainboard. He put the first plate down on the center of the table. As he turned his back for another, there was a loud crash. The first plate was in smithereens on the floor. As both men watched, Larry put a second plate down on the center of the table. The dish slid rapidly toward the edge, as if being pushed, and smashed on top of the first one.

As they stood there, incredulous, a long handmade nail flew out of the kitchen window frame and bounced onto the middle of the table. The nail was old, but in good condition. Had it simply fallen out, it would have landed on the sill below, but it had shot out of place, landing a good three feet from the window. Ten minutes later they heard the latch on the front door click down, and the door swung open of its own accord.

Malcolm and Larry ate out that night.

The foul smell in Malcolm's room and the periodic cold spot continued, but the men had no further trouble with objects flying and sliding of their own accord. Larry and Malcolm moved the candlestick down under the couch the next morning, where it stayed until they moved out the following May.

MISS
PHEBE
BEADLE

Rita Goss, of Main Street, is convinced that she shares her house with Miss Phebe Beadle.

"Miss Beadle had gone to Vassar, and she taught school on Nantucket for many years. She loved children, and was a warm, spontaneous kind of person. She lived in the house for eighteen years, from 1915 until her death in 1933. The schoolteacher was known to do unconventional, slightly risqué things; one Nantucketer told me, in a scandalized tone, that she was even seen sunbathing once or twice in her swimsuit on the widow's walk. I was delighted.

"Right after I bought the house, I had a strange experience. I had locked it up during the middle of the day and gone to do an errand. I returned to find the front door unlocked and slightly ajar. No one else on the island, that I knew of, had a key to the house. As I stepped in, I heard someone playing the piano. This was no faint tinkling of notes; it was the regular tone of someone at the keyboard. I was so startled that afterward I couldn't remember what the melody was, but I do remember that it was cheerful and pleasant-sounding.

"I stood for a moment in the doorway, wondering what I should do. Then, telling myself that on Nantucket the intruder couldn't be anyone too terrifying, I peeked around the corner to the parlor. As I did, the music stopped abruptly. The piano bench was vacant. When I got over my initial surprise, I walked through the entire house from room to room. Sure enough, I was alone.

"I asked around, trying to find out about the people who had lived there before me. The house was built about 1830 by a member of the Coffin family. Of course, no one now living could personally remember much about the people who owned the place before 1900, but of all the tenants I heard stories about, Miss Phebe Beadle sounded the most congenial. I have no idea who or what was really playing the piano, but I like to think it was she. Perhaps it was just her way of inviting me in, of telling me that I was welcome in her house."

A R E D
F R I E N D

"I was living alone in the house, and slept in the downstairs bedroom. I was awakened one night by a brilliant red light shining across my bed. I thought perhaps there had been an accident on the road; the light looked like the red beam cast by a police car or ambulance."

Bill Armstrong is a painter and former resident of Nantucket who now lives in Manhattan. During the winter of 1976 he rented a house in Polpis that then belonged to Prentice Claflin. The Claflins had moved to a smaller house for the winter. In an even, dry tone, Bill continued:

"I got up and went to the window. I looked out. I looked away, closing my eyes, and then looked out again. There, standing on a little porch outside the house, was a woman. She was bright red. She looked the way someone does under a red spotlight on stage. She was solid, but I knew from the red glow of her body that she wasn't real. I mean, I knew she wasn't alive. I found myself thinking, as if in slow motion, 'She's a ghost. A red ghost. I'm seeing a red ghost of a woman.' I don't know why I wasn't terrified, but I felt quite calm. She was about forty years old, and was wearing conservative, simple clothing that I couldn't date. I noticed that her dress was dark, although I don't remember the length, and that she had dark hair. She stared right into my eyes. Her expression was impassive, emotionless. She wasn't tragic and she wasn't threatening. I didn't feel at all the way I would have expected to feel when looking at a ghost. After we had faced each other for something like a minute, she began to fade, becoming fainter and fainter, and finally vanished altogether. I got back into bed and went to sleep.

"I saw her three more times. She always appeared at night outside the house. She was outside my bedroom window every time but one, when I saw her standing out in back, near the driveway. She was dressed the same way each time, and always looked right at me. I came to think of her as, well, a watchful friend. Maybe it's just that I was living alone and knew that if I didn't simply accept her I'd be so terrified that I'd have to move out.

"There were three or four other times when I couldn't see her but knew she was in the house with me. Once, in the evening, I was watching television downstairs and began to hear the sounds of a party coming from the empty dining room. People were laughing and talking, and I could hear the clink of china and glasses. I got up and looked into the room, but, as I suspected, there was nothing visible going on. Not knowing what else to do, I tried to ignore it and went back to my program.

"One night I had just gotten into bed, and was lying there thinking, when suddenly I knew she was in the room with me. This is probably the strangest of all my encounters with her, for she sat down on the edge of the bed. I actually felt the bed go down under her weight, although I couldn't see her. I don't know what got into me, but after a few moments I held up the covers and said, 'All right, get in!' With that, she stood up and was gone.

"An odd thing happened one night when my ex-wife stayed in the library. I forget now why she did, but it was late, I had a bunch of guests in the house, and I remember her sleeping on the sofa in there. Prenny Claflin had an impressive collection of books which covered most of one wall. In the middle of the night, with no warning, the entire wall of books flew from the shelves and crashed on the floor. It woke us all up. It was violent and inexplicable. No person could ever have flung all those books out at once without knocking down the wall. My ex-wife and I were in the midst of a complicated divorce at that time, and some of my friends have since remarked that the red woman was probably commenting on my ex-wife's presence in the house.

"I told Patty and Prenny and various friends about the things that went on that winter, but the Claflins said that they had never felt or seen anything abnormal in the house. One night, as we were sitting around talking, someone suggested that we try a seance. None of us had had any experience with such things, but it sounded intriguing, so several nights later a bunch of us, including Patty Claflin and a musician named John Houshman, sat down around the dining-room table with a Ouija board. The first thing we did was to ask if someone was there. The answer was spelled right out: YES. I don't think we had really expected it to work. Our next question was whether she needed help. Again the answer was YES. At that point Patty said she was beginning to feel uncomfortable, and she got up and went into the living room to sit by the fire. After she left, John also began to look nervous, and left to join Patty. The rest of us closed the door and continued.

"The next question we asked was, 'Is there anyone here who can help you?' The answer was spelled right out: BILL. At that point I began to feel funny, being the only Bill in the room, and decided it was time to break up the session. We talked about what had happened. I think we all felt a little shaky.

"We joined Patty and John, and I explained that the ghost had asked for help from 'Bill,' and that I had then gotten cold feet and put the Ouija board away for the night. Patty said, after a shocked pause, 'Well, we just heard her leave!' She and John had been absorbed in a conversation when they both heard a back door in the corner of the living room open and then slam shut. The door, in actuality, remained closed the entire time. They then heard footsteps clumping up what seemed to be a staircase running up the outside wall of the house. When the footsteps reached the second floor, Patty and John heard another door being yanked open and slammed shut. Both had sat, transfixed, listening to the sounds of the steps thumping diagonally up the outside wall. No stairs run up the outside of the house, and there is no door at the top opening onto the second floor. The house was built about 1830, and there is no structural indication of such a staircase or of such a door upstairs.

"And that's about it. My lease on the house ended soon after that, and I moved back to New York. I love Nantucket, but there were a few too many strange goings-on there. One only needs one such red friend in a lifetime."

ANCIENT
HISTORY

"I don't have much to tell you, really. I'm the kind of person who just hates publicity and, quite honestly, I'd be glad if you didn't think this was enough of a story to write up. Well, let's see. What? You'll have to look right at me when you say something, because I hate using my hearing aid and seldom do.

"My husband and I bought the house thirty years ago. We knew that it had belonged to a woman who was very active in Nantucket politics during the American Revolution, but that was about the extent of our historical knowledge of the building. Some years ago, I read up on all the details of her life, and she was quite a character, as you probably know. At any rate, we bought the house to enjoy and live in, and we've never dwelt on its background.

"Of course, what I'm going to tell you is all ancient history now; these things happened during our first couple of years in the house. I was staying here alone one summer with our two children; one was five, and one was still in a crib. My husband came home when he could on weekends.

"I wasn't the bravest soul in the world, at least not at that time, and although I never locked the house, I never quite relaxed, either. I was reading in bed one night when I heard a door slam. I froze and listened. I tried to read again, turning the pages quietly so as to hear – and, probably, so as not to be heard. Then I got a grip on myself, and said to myself firmly, 'Now, you're a grown woman with two little children. You should get up and check on that door, and close it if it has blown open.' So, rather timidly, I got up and walked out of my bedroom, through that door there, and into this room.

"I was standing a couple of feet from where you're sitting, right there at the edge of the rug, when I saw a woman walk through the dining-room door. She took a couple of steps and stopped opposite me. My first desperate thought was that it was some kind of optical illusion or shadow, or that a light outside was casting a strange reflection of my own body. I remember my neck went stiff as a board. I slowly turned my head, just a fraction of an inch, to see, with the corner of my eye, whether the shade was up on the window behind me. It wasn't. Besides, I was in pajamas and had curly shoulder-length hair, and she was in a long skirt with her hair either short or pulled back in a bun. She was no reflection. I was absolutely rigid with terror. She was opaque; I couldn't see her features or the details of her shirt, but I could make out the shape of her head and the long skirt. I remember thinking that if I reached toward her I wouldn't be able to feel anything, that my hand would go through her. I suppose all this happened very quickly, but it seemed like it took forever. I was right next to a standing lamp, and I finally moved and switched the light on. As soon as I did, she disappeared. Hooph! It still gives me chills to talk about this.

"I told my husband about her, and of course he thought I was imagining things. He's a physicist, and the last person to believe in such an occurrence. One night, however, I had heard him rustling the covers and sighing and turning over heavily, but I didn't completely wake up. The next morning I asked him what had been wrong. He said in a grumpy voice, 'I saw your friend. She stood right in the doorway.'

" 'Oh!' I said. 'What did you do?'

" 'What in heck do you think? Turned over and went back to sleep!' He still hates to admit that he ever saw her, and will sometimes tell people, if it comes up in conversation, that he never did.

"A couple of other little things happened, but again, they're hardly spectacular and you might not want to write them up. One was that over there, by the fireplace, we had a stack of newspapers with an inverted metal bucket on top of it and two rubber toys on top of that. My five-year-old girl, who had a very matter-of-fact, direct approach to things, asked me when I went into her room one morning what all the rustling of papers in the living room the night before had been. I stuck my head into the living room and saw the oddest sight. The bucket and toys had been placed to one side of the fireplace, and the papers had been folded and set up, in sections, as little tents all over the room. So *that* was weird, but really rather silly.

"The only other thing that happened had to do with water. We had terribly rusty water in the house when we first moved in. For a couple of summers, all our white clothes turned beige or brown, the children's hair took on orange highlights, and I finally gave up and bought brown towels and sheets. Well, my little daughter called me one morning and said that the end of her bed was wet. I went into her room, and there was, indeed, a big rusty water spot on her bedspread. The window by the end of her bed was wide open, and the screen had been pulled all the way up. It looked as if someone had opened the window, yanked up the screen, and poured a bucket of our rusty water on the bed. That was when I went around the house and nailed down all the first-floor screens.

"So that's really all that happened. I'm afraid you've come all the way out here for nothing. Oh, yes, and we and our guests have heard footsteps clumping around upstairs quite a few times when there was no one up there. I always felt slightly embarrassed to have to explain to startled visitors that it was just the ghost."

A SMELL
OF ROSES

"**I**t was in the winter of '78–'79 that all this happened. Now, I'm the kind of person who will find a rational explanation for an experience if it's at all possible, and I never pay any attention to the random bumps and creaks one always hears in an old Nantucket house. But I would describe what went on that winter as a prolonged exchange between me and something in the building.

"The house made me nervous. I felt that I had to let it know that I was friendly and uncritical, but that I wasn't about to let anything alarm me or push me out. I'm a firm believer in the idea that buildings do have personalities."

The young woman talking is an artist. She requested that her name not be used.

The house, in the center of town, is said to have been moved there from Capaum Pond around 1720. It was owned by Gardners, Barretts, Coffins, Mitchells, and Eastons, and has housed, among others, a mariner, a block-maker, a cooper, two noted silversmiths, and a successful whaling merchant.

"I was living alone in the house that winter. I began to notice an occasional strong whiff of roses. It was a localized scent, as if I had walked right up to someone wearing rose cologne. The odor was sickly sweet and extremely concentrated. It was usually in one of the rooms downstairs, although I smelled it once in my bedroom.

"I can't tell you what a strange sensation it is to smell something as immediate and as heavy as rose perfume when there is no possible physical explanation for it. There was something horribly sweet and sentimental and old about it, something that brought to mind Dickens's Miss Haversham. I tried to be matter-of-fact about the scent and not let it scare me. But really! Imagine being alone in an eighteenth-century house on a windy February night and suddenly smelling roses from an invisible source. It wasn't easy. And it wasn't just me; friends visiting me at the house smelled it too. Occasionally, two or three people would be in one room, and we would all become aware of it. Sometimes it would be in one particular spot and someone would stumble into it, so to speak, and call the others. After several months, the smell, when it was present, seemed to be softening. It didn't have the same cloying intensity to it. I can't help thinking that my determination not to let it frighten me had something to do with its disappearance. It came less and less frequently, and finally stopped altogether.

"A funny thing once happened upstairs in my bedroom. I was sleeping one night when I was awakened by loud thumps and bumps. It sounded as if a large bird were flying around and flapping against the walls of the room. It was an agitated, frantic sound. I didn't get out of bed, but I could tell that there was nothing visible causing the noise. I think I said something that I hoped was soothing to the empty air, but the sounds continued. I remember hearing fire engines in town as I lay awake listening to the thumps. I fell asleep before the noise stopped, and found out the next morning that Zero Main Street had burned down in the night. It was one of the worst fires in an old Nantucket building in years. Perhaps there was some connection between the frantic sounds in my room and the fire, but I wouldn't know what it meant even if there were!

"I try to be sensible about all this. When you think of it, it would be strange if there were no human residue, no remnants of lives, in these old houses. Layers of living haven't been swept away here as they have in most modern communities; Nantucket is still quiet and isolated in the winter, and her history is her great strength.

"I think that the smell of roses and the flapping sound were something in the ongoing past of the house that I happened to bring out by my presence that winter. Something invisible was there and I was there, and we crossed paths."

Sometimes it would be in one particular spot
and someone would stumble into it . . . .

Marianne Giffin

Blue Balliett was born in New York City. After graduating from Brown University in 1977, with a degree in Art History, she moved to Nantucket in January 1978, intending to stay only a few months. Six years later, she and her husband, William R. Klein, are still there. During the summer months Ms. Balliett runs an art gallery, and in the off season she compiles title abstracts and does research for the Nantucket Historical Association.